CAMPUS CHAINSAW MASSACRE

CAMPUS CHAINSAW MASSACRE

A SATIRE

The Medway Chronicles 1

Errol Blackadder

To The Book Club

CONTENTS

ACKNOWLEDGEMENTS

Special thanks must go to the members of the Book Club – Kim, Lionel, Martin, and Rob. They encouraged me to get started, although they may be regretting that now. Thanks also to other patient and generous readers, including Alex, Chris, Clare, David, Fran, Garth, Henry, Jodie, Karen, Lizzie, Lorna, Nathan, Nikki and Stephen. As ever, my greatest debt is to Sue, who not only read the novel but put up with its author.

1

GOLDFINGER
AND MURDO

It was a surprise to everyone when, at a meeting of the governing Council of Leichardt University, the Vice-Chancellor suddenly made a loud choking sound and pitched forward onto the table, stone dead. Now, I know what you're thinking, but this is not a whodunnit. Professor Pound died of natural causes – a massive heart attack, it was later established. He had not looked well for some time, and there had been warning signs, apparently. This story is about what happened next.

The Chancellor, Sir Aurelian Goldfinger, looked on in horror. A short, porcine man in a grey business suit, Goldfinger was a lawyer and businessman, a former chairman of the Venal Corporation, a huge oil and gas company which specialised in generating greenhouse gas emissions. He owed his knighthood to one of the bizarre 'captain's picks' of one of Australia's more regrettable prime ministers, who had revived the practice of creating knights and dames in the

Order of Australia. Even his own party soon realised how unpopular this was and had got rid of both the practice and the prime minister. But Goldfinger continued in his new pomp.

Now, however, Pound's demise confronted Goldfinger with the serious problem of finding a replacement Vice-Chancellor. It was the Vice-Chancellor, after all, who was the CEO of the university, in charge of driving forward the program of reform it so desperately needed. The Chancellor was a mere figurehead, like a ceremonial head of state.

Well, in reality Goldfinger was much more than that. It was essentially his program of reform that Pound had been appointed to push through. The program rested on a single dogma: neoliberalism. The free market should be acknowledged as the model not just for the economy but for most human activities and relationships. Obviously, this included spheres commonly assumed by the dim-witted to be the responsibility of the state, such as health care and education. In the fullness of time, market efficiencies and freedoms should be extended to all spheres, such as friendship, love, religion and so forth. Of course, myopic sentimentalists would begin to get upset at this point; that was in the nature of myopic sentimentalists. But perhaps the greatest innovation of neoliberals was to realise that in order to promote the market it wasn't enough for government to get out of the way; indeed, government was essential because the market needed to be actively promoted, by force if necessary. This is where Goldfinger saw his personal mission. Those who were fortunate enough to possess a clear, unsentimental view of things – those like Goldfinger – had to expand the jurisdiction of the market whether people liked it or not. Leading the *demos* to water was not sufficient, it had to be *made* to drink.

Goldfinger had chosen Pound to prosecute these principles at Leichardt. Pound had been about to step up the campaign when he was carried off. Or had he? Pound had recently betrayed signs of squeamishness that did not bode well. Goldfinger didn't like to put the matter in such crude terms, but perhaps the demise of Pound was not wholly tragic. Maybe it presented an opportunity to appoint someone less inclined to flinch from the necessary hard decisions.

The position had to be advertised, and the call attracted the usual range of applicants. There was, for example, Professor Philip Neptune, the distinguished astrophysicist from Sydney, Professor Egon Zitzlaff, a philosopher who ran the University of Klotz-am-Rhine, and Professor Harold Differend, a leading postmodernist theorist of literature from the UK.

There was also the internal candidate, Roy Beadle. Beadle was currently the Acting Vice-Chancellor, stepping up from his usual job as Deputy Vice-Chancellor (Academic) after the death of Pound. A distinguished political scientist, Beadle had been head of Leichardt's Politics department back in the 1990s, then the director of research for the Faculty of Non-Sciences, before becoming a Deputy Vice-Chancellor. The DVC Academic was, essentially, the second in command of the university after the Vice-Chancellor. People had always said Beadle was destined to become Vice-Chancellor in due course, and he had only just been pipped at the post by Pound last time. He would have hopes, maybe expectations, of securing the permanent job.

But Goldfinger wasn't impressed by any of them.

'The trouble with these people,' he confided to his wife Barbara, 'is they're all cut from the same cloth.'

'You mean they're all men,' said Lady Goldfinger.

'No, they're all academics. Too caught up in their own intellectual worlds, too inclined to quibble over principles, too obsessed with faded ideals instead of facing up to cold realities. The scientists aren't so bad – at least they deal in facts – although even they need sound business guidance. The people from the humanities and social sciences – the non-sciences – are completely insufferable. All that bleating about values and identities. The world doesn't owe them a living. Really, if we could liberate university management from the academics it would be a much better place.'

'But surely, the University is an academic institution, so it has to be led by an academic.'

'I thought you'd say that,' said Goldfinger. 'I'm not so sure. I think what's more important is that we find someone dynamic and determined enough to do what has to be done. Someone prepared to break a few heads if necessary.' With a sigh of frustration, he continued to leaf through the applications, searching for the champion who must be out there somewhere.

***

'Aurelian, can't you leave this Leichardt business alone for a while,' said Lady Goldfinger. 'You've been working on it for days now. And we're due at the Bushes by seven.'

'Yes, dear. I'm just getting ready now.'

Lady Barbara was right. It had been days and Goldfinger was still no closer to his goal. He'd reviewed stacks of candidates and they were all hopeless – bookworms, geeks, wonks, nerds, winners of absurd prizes, recipients of undeserved honours. Who needed these losers? He did need some distraction. Fortunately, on Saturday night there was to be a diverting dinner party given by his friend Trevor 'Coalface' Bush, the mining magnate. Goldfinger could forget about vice-chancellors for a few hours and think about other things.

At the front door of Coalface's enormous house, Goldfinger and Lady Goldfinger were met by a maid who took their coats and ushered them into a reception room. From a throng of guests, Coalface emerged to greet them.

'Goldy, good to see you, mate! And Barbara, a pleasure as always.'

'Evening, Coalsy, you're looking well,' said Goldfinger.

'Well, I can't complain. The PM does pretty much what I tell him these days, so wealth and job creation can continue unimpeded. But look, there's someone I want you to meet.'

Following Coalface, they came to a knot of guests at the centre of which was an Australian sporting legend. The features were unmistakable: the chunky, bear-like body, the thin-lipped mouth that, when not fixed in a cold, reptilian smile, had launched a thousand sledges. And, of course, there were the eyes: oddly large, round and protruding like saucers. They gave their owner, in repose, a bovine appearance.

It was Murdoch ('Murdo') McMurdo, former captain of the Australian test cricket team.

'Goldy,' said Coalface, 'I'd like you to meet Murdo.'

'Pleased to meet you, mate,' said Murdo, affably extending one of the large paws that had snagged so many slip catches.

For Goldfinger, this was a rare treat. He had never met Murdo but, as an avid cricket follower, was of course familiar with the famous career. 7,000 test runs at an average of 50 placed Murdo among the top Australian batsmen of all time. He had played 96 tests, 45 of them as captain. As captain he had a win ratio of 70%, including victory in three consecutive Ashes series.

Murdo had achieved all this with raw talent, hard work, and a very broad streak of ruthlessness. As a batsman he acquired a reputation for running out his partners: in any running mix-up, it was seldom Murdo who made his way back to the sheds. At a time when bowlers were discovering the new art of reverse-swing, Murdo pioneered a batting innovation that became known as 'reverse-farming' of the strike. While higher-order batsmen traditionally protect the tail by facing most of the bowling, Murdo would manipulate the strike so that the opposite occurred, the tailenders being obliged to protect Murdo. He justified the practice by arguing that his was the more valuable wicket. Of course, there was some precedent in the form of the 'night-watchman' institution, where a lesser batsman will be sent in late in the day to preserve better batsmen for the following day. But

Murdo thought that the principle should be extended to all occasions, at any rate when he was batting. So, for example, when the England fast bowler Alf Dobbs took 8/29 against Australia at Lord's, Murdo somehow contrived to be at the non-striker's end whenever Dobbs was bowling. His 32 not out, out of a total of 65, was hailed as a heroic masterpiece.

As a captain, Murdo regarded the opposition not so much as opponents to be defeated as vermin to be crushed, humiliated and eradicated. The goal was not merely victory but the 'mental disintegration' of the other side. To this end he raised the practice of sledging to a pitch of intensity not previously seen. On Murdo's watch, the traditional, formulaic remarks about people's wives and mothers were supplemented by real information obtained from private investigators, which included accurate reports not only of extramarital goings-on but also of drinking, betting and pornography habits, account balances, and the whereabouts of children. Within his personal sledging repertoire Murdo showed a particular liking for the 'send-off', where a stream of abuse is directed at the back of a batsman who has been dismissed as he walks off the field. The send-off had an especial appeal for Murdo because there was no come-back, at least at the time. There might be retaliation later, when he had finished batting himself, but by that time he expected to have been so successful that no send-off would have any effect on him. On the other hand, if Murdo was sledged when he was feeling more vulnerable he was apt to become extremely indignant, claiming that this kind of treatment 'crossed the line' between harmless 'banter' of the kind in which he engaged and something less sportsmanlike. Critics questioned where exactly this line was to be found and suggested that, for Murdo, 'banter' was whatever he dished out and 'crossing the line' was whatever the opposition came up with in reply. But whatever the ethical subtleties of the issue, it had to be conceded that, all things considered, Murdo's sledging and sending off practices were highly successful. Several England players, after tangling with Murdo and his teams, never played again, some passing their days as gibbering wrecks in mental homes. Umpires who displeased Murdo suffered the same fate.

Murdo's take-no-prisoners approach did eventually get him into serious trouble. Trying to recover a losing position in a test in the West Indies, he decided, against the rules, to manipulate the surface of the ball by using a piece of sandpaper. Always under the microscope himself, he delegated the task to one of the dispensable new boys, the young opener, Byron Scape. Scape was spotted by the umpire, a ball-tampering scandal erupted and that was the end of Scape's international career.

Murdo survived, however. He publicly denied that Scape was following his orders and took no responsibility. Scape never informed on him. It was apparent that Murdo had done some deal with Scape but no-one ever found out what it was – although it was rumoured that the astonishingly lucrative Indian Premier League contract that Scape soon picked up with the Chennai Checkbooks had something to do with it. Everyone knew what Murdo had done, but his wrongdoing could not be proved. With the help of a swarm of lawyers, he continued as captain.

Murdo also had a tangled love-life, or at least sex life. He had two children with his first wife, Tonya, before going over the side with the wife of his team-mate 'Tadger' Jones. That episode ended both marriages. He then married the television journalist Sharon Prenupple. That ended in acrimony when he briefly took up with the Hollywood starlet, Alopecia Merkin. Something similar happened with his third wife, Shannon, who later described Murdo as 'a disgusting chauvinist pig.' Since then, there had been a succession of girlfriends, all enthusiastically tracked in the tabloid press and women's magazines.

For Goldfinger, this record was entirely admirable. Hadn't Machiavelli himself said that 'if a prince wants to maintain his rule he must learn how not to be virtuous'? Moreover, if the prince has to act viciously, he should, if possible, get others to do his dirty work for him so they get the blame if things go wrong. For once, a philosopher who knew what he was talking about. Even Murdo's extra-marital peccadillos were evidence of the kind of flexibility – 'agility' was the word people used now – recommended by the great Florentine realist. In short, Murdo exhibited, in subtle combination, just those qualities that Goldfinger would like to see in Leichardt's vice-chancellors. If only he could find someone with comparable mettle!

Goldfinger prevailed on Coalface to seat him next to Murdo at dinner, and Coalface was happy to oblige. The Chancellor looked forward to some cricketing anecdotes that would transport him from the worries of Leichardt. Perhaps he would get to hear about the 'sledge of the century' when

Murdo had informed some hapless South African who had just missed a catch that he'd 'dropped the World Cup.' Or Murdo's threat to England's number 11 batsman that he should 'get ready for a broken arm.' Or his decision to declare the innings closed when his old friend and rival Tadger was on 99, followed soon after by getting the selectors to drop Tadger for not scoring enough centuries.

But it turned out that Murdo was equally intrigued by Goldfinger and wanted to talk about the world of the university. Even during his time as a test cricketer Murdo had been known as the scholar of the team, with his B. Comm. in Business Management from the University of Mallacoota. After he retired from cricket he pursued his studies further, travelling on a scholarship to the University of Alabama, Lynchburg, where he took an MBA. This prepared him for the public relations start-up that made his initial fortune, from which he went on to hostile take-overs and asset stripping.

'What gets me about universities,' said Murdo as he gnawed on a spatchcock, 'is their ridiculous inefficiency. All that energy wasted on people going off in different directions when everyone should be pulling together as a team. That's how we won three consecutive Ashes series. We didn't do that by letting everyone have goals different from the team's goals. Blokes not contributing to the team's goals should be dropped. That's what I did with the teams I captained. Remember what happened to Tadger.' Murdo chuckled at the recollection. 'There's no room for sentimentality if you want to win.'

Goldfinger was thrilled anew. This is my kind of man, he thought. More than this, the germ of an idea was forming in his mind. Why not? The man is a leader. He knows how to get results and he's not distracted by sentiment. He has the kind of public celebrity instantly recognisable in Australia. Of course, the usual carpers will say that cricketers can't be vice-chancellors, but that's nonsense. If Imran Khan can be prime minister of Pakistan, Murdo can lead Leichardt. He's exactly the man I want.

Murdo took some persuading, but after a two-week siege Goldfinger succeeded. He had piqued Murdo's interest, presenting him with a new challenge at the head of an institution that desperately needed him. It may also have helped that Goldfinger offered Murdo an annual salary of $1.2 million. In the old days, Vice-Chancellors at Leichardt had been paid according to a formula that gave them 42% more than the top-ranked professor. This gap had gradually widened until the late Professor Pound had earned more than five times the salary of the top professoriate, becoming the first Leichardt Vice-Chancellor to reach the million-dollar mark. Now Murdo would do better still: his salary would buy six top professors. It was twice as much as the salary earned by the heads of the best universities in the US or UK (Leichardt was ranked around number 20 in Australia). It was twice as much as the salary of the Prime Minister of Australia, or the President of the United States. Well, you had to pay top dollar to get the best people.

Murdo's application came in and, after a friendly interview, Goldfinger rammed it through the Council. The new Vice-Chancellor would be Murdo McMurdo.

2

MEDWAY

Oblivious to Goldfinger's machinations and Murdo's windfall, Geoffrey Medway, professor of political philosophy and dean of the School of Social Studies at Leichardt University, was having breakfast at home with his wife, Sarah.

'While you're at work today, Geoffrey,' said Sarah, 'I'll try to dust your hut.' The 'hut' was her name for Medway's study, because when he went in there it was as if he'd gone to a hut at the bottom of the garden, cut off from communication with the rest of the house. Sarah had recently retired from thirty years of high-school teaching and had assumed nearly all the housekeeping duties. Medway, never overactive in that department, had not objected.

'I can only say I'll do my best, and that will be pretty limited,' Sarah continued. 'I'll have to navigate round the piles of books, which are absolutely everywhere. Every time I go in, there seem to be more. Are you sure they don't somehow mate and multiply during the night?'

'I'm sorry about the books, dear,' replied Medway, 'but they're the tools of my trade. If I was a mechanic, I'd need wrenches and what-not. I'm an academic, so I need books.'

'Don't people get ebooks these days? Ebooks don't take up any room. And I've even heard it's possible to borrow books from libraries.'

'We've been over this, dear. I like hard copies I can hold in my hand, and I like to annotate them.'

'Oh, yes, I'd forgotten. But do you really need quite so many? What about that idea we discussed of getting rid of a book for every book you add? At least that would stabilize things.'

'I've tried, but it's difficult. All the books I get, I get for a reason, and the reason doesn't go away just because I need another book.'

Medway had indeed tried the 'one-in-one-out' scheme and it was indeed difficult. He'd got as far as setting aside some piles that might conceivably be sold or (more likely with academic books) given to charity. But then, when he sat down to go through them more carefully, he'd almost always found something interesting in them and couldn't bear to let them go. Opening the book was fatal. There was also the worry that, even if he judged that, here and now, he could do without the book, that was only for the present. What if he found he needed it later on? There's nothing more frustrating than finding you want a book that you had two weeks before but then sent to the Rotary Bookshop.

'Just try, Geoffrey, that's all I ask.'

'All right, I'll have another go at the weekend. But now I must be off to the tarpit.'

Postponing the book question gave Medway a feeling of mingled relief and guilt, like someone putting off a visit to the dentist. He gathered up the papers and books he needed for the day and shoved them into his backpack. Kissing Sarah, he wished her a nice day and went out to the car.

***

Another working day began at Leichardt. Medway arrived at his deanery, a large office on the west side of the building, Hayek South. He had a meeting with the Executive Dean and the other deans at 9.30, but there were a few minutes before he needed to be on his way. Greeting his PA, Astrid, he sat down behind his desk, turned on the computer to check his emails, and looked out over the adjacent Carpark 13. Not for the first time he reflected that moving in here had been a backward step, aesthetically. His previous office on the south side of the building had a gorgeous view of a stand of gum trees, through which he could see the sea in the distance. Now he saw nothing but grey asphalt divided by white lines into parking bays. Each of these had recently been fitted with a small, domed sensor, the purpose of which was to detect the presence of a car on some computerised ticketing system that had not yet been activated.

Speaking of surveillance, one advantage of his view of the carpark was that he could see who was coming and going at all times of the day without being seen himself. It was like being a guard in the panopticon, Jeremy Bentham's design for a model prison in which, from a central tower, the guards would be able to keep the prisoners under surveillance at all times without themselves being visible. Similarly, Medway could observe his staff as they came and went, and he still derived from this a certain guilty pleasure.

From the deanery, moreover, he could also see his own car. Before becoming a dean, he'd been like every other member of staff, parking as best he could on a first-come-first-served basis. Since he was not a morning person, this meant, more often than not, that by the time he arrived he had to park in a section known as 'Ultima Thule' because it was so far from Hayek South. But now, as a middle-sized cog in the administration, he was entitled to a reserved spot in Carpark 13.

Yes, he had come a long way. He had arrived at Leichardt over twenty years earlier, armed with an Oxford D. Phil. in political philosophy, one published book on John Stuart Mill, and five years of teaching experience in the United States. He was now sixty, his hair was grey and his eyesight poor. Although his chest size was satisfactory, a reward for regular swimming, he was of no more than medium height, he was obliged to wage a permanent losing battle against middle-age spread, and his spindly legs were a constant disappointment. As were his facial features. He would have liked the kind of aquiline highlights – the hooked nose, chiseled cheekbones and jutting chin – that suggested someone you wouldn't like to mess with. Instead, there was a gentle softness to Medway's facial topography, blue eyes looking warily onto the world above full cheeks, a dimpled chin resting peacefully on the hammock provided by another chin. He tended to be quiet and thoughtful, his voice was not powerful, and he did not care for speaking over the top of other people, or for public speaking in general. People encountering Medway were usually left thoroughly unthreatened.

As befitted a good academic, he had done some research before he arrived at Leichardt. The University was the city's second, founded in the 1960s as part of a new wave of Australian tertiary institutions made possible by the post-war prosperity. It was named after a heroic 19th-century explorer who had gone off into the central desert and never been seen again – perhaps an unlikely hero for an institution seeking knowledge, but there it was. Another curious point was that the explorer's name was actually spelled 'Leichhardt', not 'Leichardt.' But by the time this was noticed all the new University's constitutional documents had been produced with the misspelling, including an Act of Parliament, so 'Leichardt' it remained.

Of middling size for an Australian university at that time, Leichardt had about 8,000 students and a reputation for dedication to social justice issues and egalitarianism, even a degree of political radicalism. In 1970 the students had famously occupied the Chifley Building, where the Vice-Chancellor and his administrators had their offices. In those days many of the academic staff had been adherents of Mao Tse Tung – almost the entire Philosophy Department had been Maoists. How that could be was mystifying to Medway, since philosophy and Maoism struck him as mutually exclusive. Philosophers ask critical questions; Maoists had an uncritical faith in the Great Helmsman. But again, there it was; it was the seventies, after all.

When he arrived, Medway was immediately charmed by the physical beauty of the place. Although the buildings were constructed according to 1960s office patterns, all concrete and glass, Leichardt was perched on a hill with spectacular views of the Pacific to the east, the CBD to the north, and the suburbs all around. The site sloped downwards from the west towards the sea and was bordered to the west and south by reserves of bushland, mainly gums and pines.

The layout of the University represented a 'tree of knowledge.' The roots of the tree, the foundations of the University, lay in a kind of town square called (at the time Medway arrived) 'the Res Publica.' This was partially enclosed by the administrative offices (the Chifley Building), the Beatrice and Sidney Webb Library, and the Student Union Building which contained the university canteen. To the east, the view from the Res Publica was unimpeded, that side consisting of a large lawn, on which students frolicked in all seasons except winter, with a central concrete plinth from which they were addressed and entertained by speakers and bands. Above the Res Publica, a broad avenue – the trunk of the tree – climbed the hill to the west as far as the Ultima Thule carpark at the very top. Branching off from the trunk were paths leading to the buildings and quadrangles of the various academic disciplines. In keeping with the wishes of Leichardt's first Vice-Chancellor, a physicist, the tree represented an epistemological hierarchy. The lower branches led on the north side to the Humanities and on the south to the Social Sciences, Law and Business – 'the lower hanging fruit', in the words of the physicist. When Medway arrived, he moved into the building that housed the Social Sciences, which was then called Curtin South. In the higher branches of the tree were Engineering and the Life Sciences, and at the very pinnacle were Physical Sciences and IT.

Things went well for Medway on the whole. Along with everyone else, he was drawn into a major conflict within the Politics department between its politics and international relations factions, a conflict resolved (or evaded) eventually by the splitting up of the department and its redistribution into two different schools. But Medway also made some good friends. The students were not hard to teach – they were less talkative than American students, but their writing was better and they were less demanding – and they gave him mostly positive evaluations. His research also flourished, eventually resulting in four single-authored books and an edited collection. In administration, he served in various capacities, culminating in his recent elevation to school dean. The University signaled its approval of his efforts by promoting him, first to senior lecturer, then associate professor, then professor. He met Sarah and they moved in together.

By the time he became a dean, however, Medway had to admit that Leichardt was no longer the cosy environment he had found when he arrived. In the old Politics department nothing much had been expected apart from competent teaching. Most people published very little, some nothing. But over the years, federal governments, regardless of party, removed more and more public funding from the universities, obliging them to turn themselves into businesses. Leichardt was no exception to this trend, painfully converting itself from a bumbling but humane institution into a machine for making money. Demands on the staff became more difficult to satisfy no matter how hard people worked.

The change of climate was reflected in an orgy of rebadging. Curtin South was renamed Hayek South. The Res Publica became known as 'Company Headquarters', usually abbreviated to 'CHQ', and its constituent buildings were relabelled too: the Chifley Building was now the Milton Friedman Building, the Webb Library became the Adam Smith Communications Hub, and the Student Union Building turned into the Client Services Centre. The Business School, hitherto located (along with Law) next to Social Sciences in Curtin North, was moved to a splendid new home, the Nozick Building, at the very top of the tree, above even Physical Sciences and IT. Law stayed where it had been, in the renamed Hayek North.

Medway felt less at home in this new world, but he also thought that, all things considered, he had not done badly on a personal level. He was not going to win a Nobel Prize anytime soon, but he was teaching and publishing well, an international authority on his subject, and a respected senior leader in the School and University. In any terms he would have to be considered modestly successful; in the context of Leichardt he was positively distinguished. It seemed that he was destined to cruise happily and productively to the end of his career. That was before Ethel arrived.

Speaking of the good lady, it was time to leave for the meeting.

3

ETHEL

It was 9.30 and Professor Ethel Korova, executive dean of Leichardt's Faculty of Non-Sciences, was presiding over the monthly meeting with her school deans. Ethel's full title was 'Vice President and Executive Dean,' in keeping with the late Professor Pound's decision to call himself not just Vice-Chancellor but 'President and Vice-Chancellor.' His reason was that his counterparts in the US did not know what a Vice-Chancellor was, thinking perhaps that they were dealing with the manager of the janitorial department. Once Pound became a President, Ethel and the other executive deans had to be Vice-Presidents. The Faculty of Non-Sciences derived its name from the policies of successive scientist vice-chancellors who had dumped into the Faculty every discipline that could not reasonably be described as a natural science. These included all the various humanities and social sciences which the scientists regarded as scarcely constituting genuine academic knowledge but which nevertheless attracted a certain kind of student. The venue for Ethel's meeting was a room dubbed by Professor Toynbee, from History, 'the Wolf's Lair.' This distinguished it from Ethel's private office, which was known by everyone except Ethel as 'the Bunker.'

Ethel was in her early fifties. Her substantial, round body was swathed in flowing garments that disguised its precise contours. From this obtruded, without the aid of any visible neck, a small head featuring a round face with dark, darting eyes. When people said things that Ethel disagreed with or didn't understand – a frequent occurrence – her eyes narrowed as if she was squinting at some tiny object in the distance. In more serious cases she would, in addition, view offenders from the corner of one narrowed eye, literally looking askance at them. Her voice was deeper than might be expected, with a hoarseness that hinted at a history of booze and cigarettes. The overall impression was of a malevolent Dame Edna.

Ethel did not usually care to spend much time with her school deans, but this meeting was special because she was so looking forward to seeing their faces when she passed on the news of Murdo's appointment as Vice-Chancellor. Sure enough, the announcement was greeted with expressions ranging from astonishment and incredulity to hilarity and delight.

'This is ridiculous,' said Professor Morpheus from Psychology. 'Sure, the man was a great batsman but how is he an academic?'

'He meets the academic qualifications for the job,' replied Ethel. 'He has two university degrees and he's done significant research as part of his business experience. But let's look at what's most important here. We don't need the Vice-Chancellor to teach, research and publish. That's your job.'

Ethel paused, looking round the table accusingly. Whatever job these losers were supposed to be doing, they were not doing it. She made an exception for Professor Morpheus, because Psychology was undoubtedly performing well. The rest of them deserved to be thrown into the Pacific.

'The job of the Vice-Chancellor,' she continued, 'is to set the direction of the university as a whole, and that means above all its business direction. Murdo is a top-class businessman who's capable of doing just that. We need to free ourselves from this medieval idea that a university leader has to be an academic.'

'I agree with Ethel,' said Professor Pinfold, the dean of the Business School, delighted to be agreeing with Ethel because he was terrified of her. 'Murdo's past may be, shall we say, a little colourful, but he's proved himself to be an exceptional business leader, which is what we need. The University is, after all, a business.'

'Maybe so,' said Medway, 'but isn't it a lot more than that? What about the pursuit of truth for its own sake? What about liberal education? What about educating citizens?'

'Thanks, Cardinal Newman,' said Ethel, indulging a mirthless rictus of amusement. 'We know all that. The point is that in our current environment the University has to prioritise its capacity for generating income. We know the government isn't going to help us. We have to help ourselves.'

'Yes, that's the reality, Geoff,' said Owen Gorthwade, dean of the School of International Studies. 'It's not pretty, but we have to acknowledge it.' Medway and Owen were old friends, having both started at Leichardt in the old Politics Department in the 1990s, but they didn't agree about everything. While Medway tended to see issues through the lens of ethical values like justice, Owen liked to strike a pose of hard-nosed realism in keeping with the kind of international relations theory he professed to believe in. Recently he had given this a commercial twist, in keeping with the broad trend of higher education policy, and had taken to repeating the phrase, 'Show me the money', whenever anyone raised any issue of any kind. This was to some extent an act: Owen was more than a little given to striking poses and saying things for dramatic effect. In truth he had a more sensitive side and believed in much the same liberal values as Medway's.

'Well, it's been my experience that what's advertised as "reality" is often what so-called "realists" want to be the case,' replied Medway. 'But all right, then, we seem to have got this Vice-Chancellor whether we like it or not. What kind of policies can we expect from him?'

'In a word, reform,' said Ethel, a glint in her eye. 'Murdo has been appointed to shake things up. Expect turbulence.'

She was tempted to add, 'And you can all eat your livers.'

***

The meeting over, Ethel returned to her office deep in the bowels of Hayek South. One of her more satisfying achievements had been the reconfiguration of the building so that the administration offices, her own in particular, were now sealed off from casual access by the academic staff. Previously, these rooms had been much like any other, located on corridors along which anyone could wander. In the old days passers-by could see the Executive Dean (or 'Head of Faculty', as he – yes, it was always 'he' in those days – used to be known) sitting at his computerless desk conferring with whichever crony had his ear for the moment. Now, however, these areas were secure behind doors requiring card-entry.

The new set-up, Ethel felt, added to the mystery and awe of her authority. It was no longer possible simply to knock on her door; people had to present themselves at the Faculty's reception area and crave audience. They would then, if permitted, be buzzed through by a card-carrying underling. The card was attached to a lanyard that the underling wore round his or her neck, like a badge of servitude. Once admitted, supplicants had to wend their way among the desks of the admin staff in the outer offices to reach the inner sanctum. Some compared the experience to entering the Labyrinth with the prospect of encountering the Minotaur at the end. They had the feeling they should be unravelling a thread – more ethical than material – so they could find their way out again.

Greeting her executive assistant, Doris, Ethel entered the office and closed the door. That prig Medway was insufferable. His pompous nonsense about truth for its own sake! And he obviously had little respect for her views. That face he pulled when she said that Murdo met the qualifications! True, in making that claim she was stretching things, but the claim was minimally true, it was the view of the University, and even if it wasn't entirely convincing Medway ought to have more respect.

He reminded her of her professor when she was a first-year criminology student all those years ago. Professor Rampling had an Oxford degree, like Medway, and a low opinion of Ethel's abilities. He had recommended that she try something other than university work. Ever since, her career had been a struggle against the Ramplings and Medways of this world, those supercilious bastards who kept questioning her views. They had no appreciation of how hard she'd had to work to rise above the working-class background of her Russian immigrant family – the drunken violence of her motor-mechanic father and the invincible ignorance of her mother, who cleaned houses for the well-off.

But she had shown them all. She had persevered and got her degrees, including a PhD. She had attached herself to successful research teams and built up an impressive record of co-publication. As she became better known, she branched off on her own, making her name as something of an iconoclast. While other criminologists took the fashionable hippy line opposing incarceration and supporting rehabilitation, Ethel stood firm on the need for punishment. Basically, she called for more people to be locked up: it was what they deserved. As time passed and her confidence grew, she began to advocate a return to not just to punishment but to corporal punishment. Her article, 'Don't Spare the Rod: A Statistical Case for Whipping', became a classic. And now, in addition to her academic influence, she had real administrative authority and was prepared to use it. If the Ramplings and Medways continued to defy her they would find they had taken on a dangerous opponent. Not only would they be defeated, they would be battered and maimed, their wrecked bodies left in the dust, their heads displayed on spikes.

Of course, it wasn't just Medway; her school deans had almost always been disappointing. Ethel always had high hopes of them when they started and was warmly encouraging, but they soon revealed levels of weakness, incompetence and disloyalty that were simply insupportable. She would then have to push them hard to do their job properly, but this would seldom have much effect in the face of their ineptitude and intransigence. Some of them showed their fragility by having breakdowns and needing to be replaced. For example, there was the inaugural dean of International Studies, a friendly, easy-going person who had been the director of a minor think-tank somewhere. Ethel had appointed him in the knowledge that he had no experience of either teaching or administration in a university but thought he would rise to the challenge. He didn't. After one especially inspiring pep talk he was found hiding under his desk.

The deans of Social Studies had been no better. Kate Cardigan, the Leichardt Distinguished Professor of public health policy, had been capable but irritating, asking awkward critical questions. Fortunately, she was only an interim appointment and went back to teaching and research at the earliest opportunity. She was followed by Karl Toxteth, a professor of social work, who had become far too assertive and had to be shown his place, causing him to flee back to the UK. Then there was another, more kindly, social worker, who Ethel was sure would be more malleable but who again turned out to have ideas of her own. She was succeeded by Diana Rex, a public policy wonk who was pleasingly driven by statistics, but who kept interpreting the numbers in questionable ways – that is, in ways at variance with Ethel's.

And now there was Medway. When Ethel had arrived at Leichardt five years before, he had started well with her. She had approved of his admin work and on that basis had made him dean of the Social Studies school. That's when things began to go downhill. Medway turned out to be one of those people who were full of tedious and self-righteous complaints about injustice and inequality. This picture was confirmed for Ethel when he sent her an email bleating about how a casual academic called Ki-Lee Bodkin had been unfairly excluded from employment by the Faculty. He was trying to arrange for her to teach her usual sociology course when he discovered that Human Resources had marked her file 'unemployable.' That label was no surprise to Ethel because she had ordered it to be placed there.

Bodkin had been doing some contract work for a research unit. Ethel was fond of the unit and its director, Derek Bluff, because, although academic snobs like Medway might say the work they performed scarcely counted as creative research (actually, he had a point there), it brought in substantial amounts of money. Bluff had determined that one of Bodkin's reports was plagiarised. Without informing her, he had passed his judgement on to Ethel, who in turn passed it to Human Resources. So, when Bodkin's teaching contract came up for renewal, it was not approved.

In his email, Medway said he'd spoken to Bodkin, who was shocked by the allegation. She confessed that she had been careless with the report, into which she had inserted some public website material as a place-holder for what she was going to write in her own words. But she denied that she had deliberately plagiarised anything. Her story was that, up against a tight deadline, she had forgotten to replace the public material with her own work when she submitted the report. She had been in a bad way at the time, trying to care for her seriously ill mother and also unwell herself. As soon as she had realised her mistake, she had got in touch with Bluff and sent him a cleaned-up version of the report. He received the revised report without further comment.

Medway's email conceded that Bodkin had made a serious mistake, but it seemed to him that, in the circumstances, she might be given another chance. Ethel's decision had been made entirely on the say-so of Bluff; Bodkin had been given no opportunity to defend herself or point to any extenuating circumstances. She had not even been told that she had been condemned. Medway said that Ethel should hear her side of the story.

Ethel did not care to be bothered with this trivia, but she agreed to let Medway come and speak to her on Bodkin's behalf. She took the precaution of first getting in touch with Gertrude Strappado, the Faculty's thin, pale, robotic Human Resources officer, to get her advice on how best to crush Medway's whining complaint. Medway had been in touch with Gertrude too, so she was well placed to advise Ethel on how to undermine him.

Ethel asked Gertrude to come to the meeting 15 minutes early, so they could go over their agreed position. By the time the meeting was due to commence, they were well prepared.

'Professor Medway's here,' said Doris on the phone.

'Thanks, but tell him to wait,' said Ethel. She was ready to start but wanted to let Medway stew outside for as long as possible.

Eventually, he was let in, and the look on his face was priceless. As soon as he saw that Gertrude was already there, and that she and Ethel had been having a private conversation, he knew Bodkin was doomed. He did his best, arguing that due process had been lacking because Bodkin had not been given a chance to be heard. He supported his view with various documents, including a timeline of events drawn up by Bodkin.

'I have concerns about this,' said Gertrude, unctuously exuding an air of profound dedication to the rules and processes of the University. 'This timeline includes events from some months ago. It's a dangerous practice to rely on claims like this reconstructed from memory.'

'But I was only following the advice you gave me,' replied Medway. 'And most of these events are reconstructed from the email record.'

'That may be,' countered Gertrude, 'but they're still questionable because they're subject to Ms Bodkin's interpretation.'

'Well, everything is subject to interpretation,' replied Medway. 'That's why we're having this conversation. The least we can do, I would have thought, is listen to what Ki-Lee Bodkin has to say. Derek Bluff seems to have decided her case without giving her any kind of natural justice. Surely …'

This was the moment Ethel had been waiting for. 'Don't blame everything on Derek,' she interrupted, affecting anger at the besmirching of Golden Boy. 'It's not Derek who's plagiarised his research, it's Bodkin.' Medway had fallen into a trap: he'd given Ethel an opportunity to switch the subject away from the real issue.

'Well, that's the allegation,' said Medway, 'but it hasn't been tested because we haven't taken account of Ms Bodkin's explanation.'

'Okay, we have now,' Ethel said. 'You've made a case for her. Pretty offensively, I have to say. My decision stands.'

Without further comment, Ethel looked away and started chatting to Gertrude again. But out of the corner of her eye she peeked at Medway, enjoying the sight of him as he sat there stunned, as if hit over the head with one of his own boring books. This was followed by an equally entertaining look of anger, as if the pathetic man was contemplating some act of violence. Finally, he passed into a phase of resignation, sadly getting to his feet, gathering up his papers and leaving the room. With opponents like this, who needed friends?

When would these people learn that, as deans, their job was not to save the world – let them fantasise about that in their ridiculous publications. Their job was to help the University to be a thriving business. If they didn't understand that, Ethel would make them understand. If they still didn't get it, she would throw them over the side; it was nothing more than they deserved. Indeed, the removal of those surplus to requirements was perhaps the most rewarding part of Ethel's job, bringing with it a degree and kind of pleasure like no other. It was what got her up in the morning.

4

THE SCHOOL

'I've written to the local council,' said Sarah at breakfast. 'A fat lot of good it will do me, but I have to do something.'

'Ah yes, what were you writing to them about?' asked Medway.

'Really, Geoffrey, I've mentioned these things often enough. Sometimes I don't think you listen to me.'

'Sorry, dear.'

'Actually, I've sent them two emails. One is about that street tree that needs cutting back. It's hanging over our fence, getting in the way of pedestrians and killing that rose I've been trying to save.'

'Of course, what was the other email about?'

'The footpath. The roots of the street tree are cracking the footpath and creating a walking hazard. In fact, there's the same problem all along the street. It's been ages since their last inadequate patch-up job.'

'True.'

'How come Primo Street has new paving on both sides and we don't? You see that kind of thing all over the suburb. One street has splendid new paving, the next one doesn't. Some have new paving on one side but not the other. What exactly is the council's maintenance plan? Do they in fact have one, or do they pull marbles out of a hat? Anyway, that's what I'm asking them.'

'A good question, and it will be interesting to hear what they say. If they're like Leichardt, they'll claim they have a plan but it's really the marbles. I must be off, I'm afraid. No rest for the innocent.'

***

This morning Medway had to chair the monthly staff meeting of the School of Social Studies. For once, he would have something remarkable to report, the appointment of Murdo. On his way to the meeting room, he wondered how many people would suffer as a result of the University's gobsmacking decision. New vice-chancellors always like to make their own mark. Even the most incremental and benign tend to fiddle with existing systems and introduce pointless innovations just to declare they've arrived. What would happen when an anomalous brute like Murdo was in situ?

Medway felt sentimentally protective of the staff. Early in his tenure as dean, when Professor Pound was still Vice-Chancellor, he had a formative experience. He had been working on a first-year course, *Introduction to Modern Ideologies*, with Nick Wedgwood-Benn, one of his younger, livelier and more sympathetic colleagues. Medway and Nick usually presented the course together, but with Medway's elevation to the deanship Nick had taken over the convening duties. Medway was still pencilled in to deliver the lectures on 'political ideas' – they were too afraid to use the word 'theory' in case it frightened the students – and Nick still politely consulted him about the design of the course. While they were settling the schedule and readings, they passed the course guide back and forth between them, annotating the parts they wanted to change.

Nick had so many things going on in his life that he was permanently overcommitted. This is probably true of all academics now, but Nick was always an especially serious case. Between his teaching, research and child-minding duties – for the last of which, from his own account, he needed a whip and a chair – he would race back and forth on his bicycle, scarcely having time to pause for a quick vegan repast of mashed yeast. Sometimes, in his understandable haste, he made mistakes.

One such mistake came to light when Nick posted the completed guide for the *Ideologies* course online. The first Medway heard of the problem was when he received an email from Roy Beadle, who had been Medway's first head of department at Leichardt and was currently Deputy Vice-Chancellor (Academic). Somehow, Nick had posted the course guide while neglecting to remove the private annotations he had exchanged with Medway. One annotation in particular had caused offence. Nick's note recommended the deletion of a reading they had used previously on the ground that it was 'too difficult for these sandal-wearers.' Personally, Medway enjoyed the Orwellian allusion, but a humourless public servant who was taking the course was deeply insulted, possibly because she was fond of sandals and resented any suggestion of anti-sandal discrimination. Since this was obviously a matter of huge public concern, she complained directly to the Vice-Chancellor, who passed the matter to Beadle.

Replying to Beadle's email, Medway apologised for the mistake and said he would have a word with Nick. But that was not the end of the matter. Later that day he received a phone call from Beadle following up his email. 'I appreciate your concern for the well-being of your staff,' said Beadle in his mumbling baritone, 'but I must insist that you speak to Nick Wedgwood-Benn in the strongest possible terms and make sure nothing like this ever happens again.' Medway was reminded of how irritating he had often found Beadle as head of department: his pedantic obsession with propriety for its own sake could be trying. There was something of the head prefect about Beadle, and in the distant past he had in fact been the head prefect of a private school downtown.

Beadle's message about Nick did have a powerful effect on Medway, but in a way opposite to that intended by Beadle. Yes, thought Medway, they are my staff and I am concerned for their well-being. Henceforth, if he erred it would be on the side of the staff rather than senior management. Rather sentimentally, he began to think of himself as the School's *pater familias*. More romantically still, he saw himself as akin to

Nicholas II in his role as *malen'kiy otets*, the 'little father' of his people.

Medway knew this attitude would probably get him into trouble, yet hoped it might not. He knew this hope was irrational but couldn't altogether extinguish it, and it persisted like a tiny voice in the background. The voice reminded Medway of the Roman practice in which an emperor or general leading a triumphal procession had a slave whispering in his ear, 'You are only a man.' Medway's voice said, 'Maybe you'll get away with it.'

To a great extent, of course, his precarious situation was his own fault. He had listened to Ethel's siren song and agreed to become dean when Diana Rex resigned. Diana said she had served her time with Ethel and could take no more. Rather than appoint a new permanent dean, which would have involved an expensive search, Ethel wanted Medway to serve an interim dean for an initial period of a year, perhaps extendable to eighteen months.

He could have refused, but he accepted Ethel's invitation. These admin jobs seemed to him to be obligations, especially if you were at the rank of associate professor or above. In this case, he also had some idea of what the dean had to do, having served as Diana's deputy. Finally, shameful to confess, the idea appealed to Medway's ego. He would be king, albeit of a limited realm, for a year or so.

The trouble was that he knew he might end up like one of those sacrificial kings, stabbed or strangled at the end of his term. This had happened to almost every dean who had worked for Ethel, and Medway saw it as a distinct possibility for him. He had never been a favourite of Ethel's – too reticent, guarded, and unforthcoming; she preferred people who would keep her entertained. Having heard that Medway had a sense of humour, she once asked him to 'Say something funny.' Not being a professional stand-up comedian – although lecturing can sometimes approximate – he couldn't think of anything. Maybe it was just as well. He would not be a favourite, but that would help to lower Ethel's expectations of him. In spite of the dangers, he thought that he might somehow, in the manner of most policy makers, muddle through. If it came to the worst, he could always return to teaching and research, which were his main interests anyway.

Gradually, however, it became clear that the dangers were greater than he'd imagined. Every school dean in the Faculty of Non-Sciences had the privilege of meeting one-to-one with Ethel every week, so Medway had the opportunity to observe her closely. What he saw was disturbing. It wasn't just that Ethel needed to manage and discipline the Faculty in accordance with the University's rules. That would have been the approach of someone like Beadle. With Ethel, it was not the rule of law but the rule of Ethel. It was personal. Those who stepped out of line – that is, those who took positions other than Ethel's – would not only be brought to heel but, so far as it was within Ethel's power, as it often seemed to be, punished and humiliated. Moreover, Ethel would positively enjoy administering the punishment and humiliation; there was a vindictive quality in her that was thoroughly disquieting. It brought to mind that character from Faulkner who 'would look forward to the times when they faulted, so I could whip them.' Meeting with Ethel was like being summoned to confer with Idi Amin. Medway began to wonder how long it would be before he would find himself suspended by hooks from the ceiling.

***

Entering the School meeting room, Medway cast his eye over the assembled staff. Good, he could see that sensible representatives were present from each of the School's component disciplines: Politics and Public Policy, Social Work, Sociology, and Women's Studies. Nigel Plume, the head of Politics, was off sick again, but no matter, his deputy, Pleonexia Self, was there. He quickly went through the routine part of the agenda before coming to the news about Murdo.

Audible gasps accompanied the announcement, followed by varied expressions of consternation and incomprehension.

'Is this a joke?' asked Kate Cardigan. Professor Cardigan was a top-flight social scientist in the traditional Leichardt mould, a proponent of social justice in the health services who ran her own research institute. She had recently been given the elite title of 'Leichardt Distinguished Professor' and awarded an Order of Australia.

'Murdo McMurdo is not an academic leader; he's not even an academic,' fumed Professor Cardigan. 'He has no experience of university administration, and there's no evidence that he appreciates the traditions of university life or the nature and value of what universities do. He's also a very dubious character, as everyone remembers from that episode in the West Indies. How can he possibly be a suitable candidate for Vice-Chancellor of Leichardt?'

'Kate is right. Is this really the best we can do?' asked Nola Corrigan, the head of Social Work. Nola called herself 'the Flamingo' because she had only one leg. Medway once carelessly used the expression, 'it will cost an arm and a leg', to which Nola replied that this was a price she could not afford. The missing leg had been removed because of cancer when she was in her early teens. Slightly built, she now hopped nimbly about with the aid of crutches, campaigning indefatigably for various causes, including national disability insurance and the Social Work discipline.

'This is the flaming limit!' yelled Millicent O'Brien-Sanchez, the Marxist head of Women's Studies, who said nothing at less than high volume, as if urging comrades to the barricades. Getting her start in the radical politics of Liverpool in the 1980s, she was described by wags as constituting a one-woman 'Millicent Tendency.' 'Since when,' Millicent thundered, 'does the University appoint misogynistic gorillas as Vice-Chancellors?'

'Hang on a minute.' A helium-powered voice, reminiscent of Donald Duck's, entered the conversation. It was Bruno Whelper, like Owen a longstanding colleague of Medway's from the old Politics department. Whelper was an expert on state politics and had built a minor reputation as a media commentator on local elections. This brought him into contact with political celebrities, giving Whelper the impression that he was close to important centres of power.

'As you know, I'm the staff rep on the Academic Caucus,' said Whelper, pausing to emphasise this impressive fact. The Caucus was a kind of chamber of review for decisions of Council. It could make recommendations but had no decision-making power of its own. 'We saw the Council's arguments in favour of Professor McMurdo, and I can tell you they were powerfully justified.'

'Really, what were the justifications?' returned Professor Cardigan.

'I can't divulge details of Caucus discussions,' Whelper replied, hinting that he was privy to highly sensitive state secrets, 'but I can assure you they were careful and well-informed. Let me just say this: it's an advantage to Leichardt to have such a high-profile person as Vice-Chancellor – sorry, President and Vice-Chancellor.'

'A high-profile laughing-stock, you mean,' said Cardigan.

'I think you have to accept,' Whelper replied, 'that we in Caucus have seen information unavailable to you. But you should also rest assured that the interests of the staff have been well served. As you know, I had the ear of the late Professor Pound. When Professor McMurdo takes office, I expect to have the same influence with him.'

'Will you be sucking his ear or some other appendage?' asked Millicent.

'Sorry, what was that?' Whelper demanded, turning towards her.

'Okay, ladies and gentlemen,' Medway interposed quickly, having seen where these exchanges went in the past, 'let's keep it clean.'

'People are right to be concerned about this,' said Pleonexia Self. A tiny, bird-like woman with grey eyes and a short but sharp beak for a nose, Pleonexia specialised in the politics of climate change, the promotion of her own interests, and the propagation of rumours.

'Murdo's business reputation is all about restructuring,' said Pleonexia. 'When he takes over a business, the first thing he does is sack everyone and make them apply for their own jobs. Only some survive. Basically, he's a hired assassin. I've heard on good authority that that's what will happen at Leichardt.' These observations were delivered with some relish, as if Pleonexia couldn't wait to see who would be assassinated, since she was sure it wouldn't be her. All her rumours were delivered with the same air of conviction and hinted at her possession of arcane knowledge, not unlike the claims of Whelper. Like the claims of Whelper, they frequently turned out to be false. This time, however, what she said possessed a grim plausibility. Medway had heard the same thing from other sources.

There was a chastened silence, then Nick Wedgwood-Benn spoke. 'I wonder if we could meet with the Chancellor and express our concerns. I'm sure Goldfinger would listen to what we say and give it some consideration.' Nick tended to believe that everyone had the same reservoir of benevolence and good faith that he had, as if Leichardt was the embodiment of a Habermasian ideal speech situation. If only there were enough meetings and they went on for long enough, Nick seemed to think, people were bound to agree eventually.

'Are you, Nick?' Medway replied, his voice jaded by experience with Ethel and others. 'We could try. I'd be willing to write to Goldfinger and ask to see him, but I doubt he'd bother even to receive me. Ethel wouldn't like it either. I'm afraid we have to remember that the University is not a democracy; our masters don't care what we think. The Murdo decision has been made and there's little we can do about it.'

***

On this sombre note the School meeting concluded and Medway returned to the deanery for lunch at his desk. He was due to conduct an annual performance review at 2 pm. Annual reviews were exhausting but Medway found them interesting because they provided a window on all the different lives and projects within the school. In line with his guiding ethos, his general approach was to try to be as positive as possible about what people were doing, no matter how challenging this might seem. Regular beatings did not seem to him to be likely to get the best out of people.

On the other hand, Medway knew that it would not be fair to the staff if he didn't say something about the increasingly demanding expectations of the Faculty and University. Everyone now had very substantial publication targets to aim at, in terms of both number and quality. Ethel wanted everyone to publish their articles in journals that were ranked at the top 'Q1' level according to the Scimago system – the name always made Medway think of a Shakespearean villain: 'O damned Scimago!' The reality was that people had very little control over this kind of outcome, since journal publication was largely a lottery. You might write a mediocre article that was waved through by sympathetic referees, or an excellent piece that was turned down because one referee was offended by your not citing their tedious work. Nevertheless, the schools were ordered to adjust their workload plan to 'incentivise' people to produce Q1s.

In order to balance all these considerations, Medway found himself giving his staff two separate pep talks. In one, the 'human' talk, he would try to empathise with their own judgements about what they thought was important. This he would put forward as his personal view. In the other, the 'institutional' talk, he would warn that following one's bliss might have costs, depending on the nature of the bliss in question. Here he would point to the official expectations. In the end, individuals would have to make up their own minds about how to weigh these demands. Like a family GP, Medway tried to be both realistic and reassuring at the same time. But it was not altogether easy to reassure even himself.

At 2 pm, Astrid ushered Fido Inkster into the room. Tall, with neat greying hair and thick-lensed glasses, Fido had briefly been a public servant before getting his first job as a public administration lecturer in the early 1980s. Apart from when he had to teach his classes, he was almost wholly nocturnal, usually arriving at the end of the day and working in his disordered office late into the night. Fido was quiet and contemplative, a bachelor who exuded the preoccupied, transcendent air of a medieval monk, and he usually showed a total lack of interest in pursuing any agenda except his own research and, to a lesser extent, his teaching. Promotion had seemed of little concern to Fido – he had taken thirty years to reach the level of senior lecturer. But Medway was aware that now, suddenly, Fido wanted to take the next step on the ladder.

'Hi, Fido, take a seat,' said Medway, gesturing towards the conference table and drawing up a chair. 'Okay. I see from the form you've filled in that you've expressed an interest in promotion to associate professor.'

'Yes, that's right. I've been a senior lecturer since I was appointed here fifteen years ago. So, I suppose it must be time I was promoted.'

'Well, I'd like to see you promoted but it's not just a matter of time served. Each level has its own profile set out in the promotion rules, and in your case there's a bit of a problem.'

'Oh, what's that?'

'Publications, I'm afraid. I know how dedicated you are to your research, and I respect that. Unfortunately, you haven't produced that many publications. I can only see four journal articles since your appointment to Senior Lecturer ten years ago.'

'Isn't that enough?'

Medway fought down the urge to ask Fido which planet he was living on. 'No, I'm afraid not. For promotion to associate professor you'd probably need about four times that number of published articles in that time. Preferably one or two books as well.'

'I see,' said Fido thoughtfully, as if hearing for the first time that he lived in a heliocentric universe.

'Of course, I know you're working on a major project.'

'I am,' said Fido, brightening as he always did when he was asked about this. 'I'm listing and classifying all significant theories of human nature, from Plato onwards.'

'Yes, I know,' said Medway. 'How's the spreadsheet going?'

'Oh, very well, thanks. I'll show you.' From a manila folder, Fido extracted three pieces of paper, each of which started as a narrow oblong but unfolded into an A3. Medway was afraid this would happen. He had seen versions of Fido's epic template before. Last time there had been only two A3s.

'As you can see, I list the theories in the left-hand column. In the corresponding columns I record the author of the theory, the main works in which it was presented, and its treatment of various themes such as power, contract, authority, fellowship, spirituality and materiality.'

Fido passed the document to Medway, who could see the multiple columns, all packed with print in tiny 8-point font. Each time he saw this creation, the columns and files seemed to have multiplied, so that the font needed to be reduced to get it all onto the page. The words were now almost unreadable by the naked eye, giving the thing a monstrous quality that brought to Medway's mind a favourite passage from Flann O'Brien: 'At this point I became afraid. What he was doing was no longer wonderful but terrible. I shut my eyes and prayed that he would stop while doing things that were at least possible for a man to do.'

'Over the three A3s, I list ninety-four theories,' said Fido proudly.

'Impressive,' said Medway. 'But what are you going to do with all this?'

Fido looked reflective again. 'I haven't really thought about that. I've been concentrating on the basic research: locating the theories, analysing them using my categories, and recording them on the spreadsheet. I need to finish this initial stage of the project before I think of what to do next.'

'But you've already got ninety-four theories here. How many more do you need?'

'Maybe another dozen or so.'

'And how long have you been doing this?'

'About twenty years.'

'Well, as I say, it's impressive,' said Medway. He was to some extent in awe of Fido's achievement, which demonstrated a huge reservoir of knowledge. On the other hand, having assembled and categorised the theories, Fido never seemed to do anything with them. The assembling was the whole enterprise. It was as if he expected that, once the theories were captured on his spreadsheet, they would speak to him without any further prompting, leading him automatically to some final insight on a level with Buddhist *satori*.

'But I do wonder,' Medway continued, searching for a way of making his message palatable, 'if it wouldn't be wise to give some more thought to where you're going with all this. What's your argument? What are you doing that's original and valuable?'

'Okay, maybe.'

'Because, as it is, it reminds me more than a little of Casaubon's *Key to All Mythologies*.' He knew he shouldn't have said that even as he was saying it, but he couldn't help himself.

'Really? That's interesting. Can you send me the reference?' That's why Medway shouldn't have said it.

'No, sorry, Fido, I didn't mean to suggest another theory of human nature for you to add to your spreadsheet. I meant … never mind, I'll explain another time.'

Fido was never going to be promoted. Ethel had taken one look at an earlier version of his spreadsheet and squinted in disgust.

'He's a bit different, isn't he?' she had commented. 'Frankly, this application is an embarrassment to the School and the Faculty. Talk him out of it.'

The 'embarrassment to the School' argument was one Medway had heard before, and he didn't care for it. People had a right to apply for promotion whether the School or Ethel liked it or not. But the brute fact was that Fido's publication record was nowhere near strong enough for the next step on the ladder.

'Fido, you can apply for promotion if you want, but my advice is that you're not quite ready. I think you should wait at least until you've published two or three more articles. Also, give some thought to what exactly you want to argue in your big project.'

'Okay, Geoff, I'll do as you suggest.'

Medway had a soft spot for Fido. His complete focus on truth for its own sake was an echo of some academic ideal that was lost in antiquity, or at any rate in the 1980s.

5

KNOWLEDGE
DELIVERY

The following day was Medway's teaching day. Although he now spent most of his time on dean matters, he still did a little teaching – or 'knowledge delivery', as it was now called – and this morning he had a lecture to give in *Introduction to Modern Ideologies*. Entering at the top of the tiered lecture theatre, he walked down to the lectern. 'Stumped' down would have been more accurate, since the aisle seemed to have been stepped in a way cunningly designed to prevent you achieving any kind of walking rhythm. One, two, bump! One, two, bump!

In position at the lectern, he commenced his ritual pre-lecture set-up. He began by popping a honey-lemon lozenge into his mouth, allowing it to coat the back of his throat. This was followed by an organising of notes and a check that all his ancillary equipment was easily reachable: watch, bottle of water, whiteboard marker. He had been doing this for years. These days he had other tasks in addition. He logged on to the lecture theatre computer, inserted his USB, found and opened the file containing his PowerPoint slides, and made sure these were properly projected on the giant screen above his head. Finally, he picked up the mobile microphone, clipped its body to his belt and the mic itself to the front of his shirt. He made sure that the mic was on by checking that the little light on its body was showing red. Unless this happened, the lecture would not be recorded and streamed on the website.

He was ready and it was time to start. Still, he paused. The image occurred to him of Hitler whipping his audience into a frenzy of expectation by keeping them waiting. He looked out over the lecture theatre, scanning from side to side and from the front row to the top of the amphitheatre. He noted a salient fact: there was hardly anyone there.

Scattered over the huge room, small knots of students were giggling among themselves and loners were playing with their mobile phones. Students seem to think that when they sit down in an auditorium they become invisible, but Medway could usually see quite clearly what they were up to, and this was especially so when there were so few of them. In between the scattered listeners there were wide open spaces. Medway had the sense that he was talking into a void.

This was what lectures were like in the brave new world of 'online delivery.' It had begun when some lecturers discovered that they could post lecture recordings on websites so their students could replay them later. The University soon made it a rule that every course must have 'an online presence', and before long this was interpreted to mean that all lectures had to be recorded and posted.

The new practice had a major advantage and an equally serious disadvantage. The advantage was that the many students who were subsisting on wages from part-time or full-time jobs were liberated from having to attend lectures in person. This was also the disadvantage. The students realised that they did not have to go to lectures anymore, so few of them did, whether employed or not. Medway and his colleagues found themselves addressing large lecture theatres with no one in them. The experience was deflating. It was especially a problem for people like Medway who designed their lectures to be interactive, since it's hard to have a conversation when there was no one to converse with.

Encouraged by these developments, the University now sought to expand into the world of *wholly* online teaching. Senior management was waking up to the fact that, beyond simply recording and posting lectures in face-to-face courses, it was possible to construct entire degrees that could be offered on the internet without the student ever having to come near the physical campus. In this way, Leichardt could sell its tawdry wares to students all over the country, indeed the world, reaching the Sami people of Lapland or the Yanomami of the Brazilian rainforest. There was obviously huge potential for making money out of this. Other universities were already doing it, and – to adapt President Kennedy and General Buck Turgidson – Leichardt could not abide an online gap!

The Master of Public Policy degree taught by the Politics and Public Policy discipline was one of the first programs to be selected for wholly online delivery. Medway accepted the task of creating an online version of one of the existing face-to-face courses which included some political theory. He was briefly taught to use an online video recording program and told to record mini-versions, each no more than 15 minutes long, of the necessary lectures. As a practical matter, this had to be done at the end of the day after all the usual teaching and administration had been completed.

So, night after night, after his usual work was completed – mercifully, this was before he became dean – Medway wrote and recorded mini-videos that would be made available, on payment of an inflated fee, to audiences across the world. These performances were agonising to a degree, since they had to take place without any of the cues or feedback offered by a physical audience. Medway stared into the computer, trying to imagine a human being somewhere in cyber-space. Perhaps the Sami would listen to him after slaughtering a reindeer, and the Yanomami would tune in while fishing for piranha. Despite the effort expended and the pain involved, the finished product did not look too exciting. Medway did not have the time to learn how to do anything fancier than display his lecture slides with a box in the bottom corner where he could be seen yelling desperately into the ether. For some reason, he could never position the box high enough on the screen to avoid looking like Kilroy peering over the top of the toolbar at the bottom.

***

Owen called. 'Have time for a coffee?' he asked.

'Sure,' said Medway.

They collected the coffee from the commercial kiosk nearest to Hayek South – the days of having instant coffee available in the staff common room were over, abolished in one of Ethel's cost-cutting drives – and walked round to a patch of dead ground at the back of Hayek South. This was where Owen and Medway often met for a break because it was one of the few remaining places on campus where Owen could smoke.

Owen had been among those who had welcomed Medway to the Politics department back in the 1990s. He later moved to Queensland to become the head of an international relations department but returned to Leichardt when the opportunity arose to become dean of International Studies with promotion to professor. After charming Ethel in the interview, he was for a time installed as a favourite. However, being Ethel's favourite tended to be a short-lived matter and Owen soon fell from grace. International Studies was the smallest school in the Faculty of Non-Sciences, and it made even less money than the basket-case Business School. According to Ethel, this was all Owen's fault. She was increasingly rude and demanding with him, calling him up at one in the morning to insist that his response to a damning review of the school be on her desk by nine am, later revealing with a smile that she did not really need it until a month later.

'So, what's been happening?' asked Medway once Owen had got his smokes out.

'The usual horrors, but some exceptional ones too,' said Owen, a cigarette now projecting incongruously from his round, boyish face. He had been born in the year the Berlin Wall was erected but looked and behaved as if permanently in his late twenties. 'You know Jose Escondido?'

'The Wuhan supremo.' Escondido was an international relations lecturer who had been given the job of running a Masters program in China, which required his presence *in situ* for about two-thirds of the year. He actually spent a good deal of this time living with his wife in Thailand, which somehow counted as being stationed in China – perhaps Ethel did not realise these were different countries.

'That's the guy. Well, Ethel has recently woken up to the fact that Jose hasn't been seen at Leichardt for two years.'

'Really? I thought the rule was that we had to report for work on campus unless explicitly given leave to be elsewhere.'

'That's the rule. But Jose got this Wuhan job, then he was awarded some study leave. Now he seems to think that the two things together entitle him to live overseas permanently. Even before I took over as dean, he hadn't been on campus for a year or more.'

'Good God.'

'For months I was sending him emails asking when he was going to return. He kept putting me off. The final straw was when he said he wouldn't be able to attend the next graduation ceremony in China because he couldn't coordinate the flights from Thailand. So, I raised the issue with Ethel.'

'Jesus, I can see where this is going.'

'Quite. Well, Ethel and I agreed that if Jose didn't attend the ceremony, he'd be subject to disciplinary measures, including severance of his contract. I also told her I'd take over the China program, which is in a complete mess anyway. Ethel agreed. Jose had been a golden boy when he'd volunteered to run the program, but now that Ethel had me, Jose was dispensable.'

'Sounds like a familiar pattern.'

'So, I emailed Jose, copying Ethel in, and told him to be at the ceremony. After that, Jose would need to return to Leichardt so his teaching program could be worked out for the coming year. He turned up to the ceremony but didn't return to campus. Where was he? He wouldn't reply to emails. Had he returned to Australia? Or gone back to Thailand? Was he dead?'

'Like Conrad's Mr Kurtz.'

'Exactly, except "he *not* dead". One night, I googled Jose's name. I found him on page 2, where he was described as an associate professor at Abu Klea University, in one of the Gulf states.'

'What!'

'Incredible, isn't it? Jose had been holding down two jobs at the same time. When Ethel discovered this, she sacked him.'

'Go, Ethel!'

'But Jose wasn't finished. He argued to the Union that he hadn't been subject to due process since he hadn't been given an annual review of progress the previous year. You have to have an annual review to give you fair warning of any problem the University finds with your work. The Union supported him, and the University told Ethel he had a case.'

'Go, Jose!'

'Yes, but then Ethel turned on me. Her complaint was, why hadn't I had a review meeting with Jose?'

'Surely, because he'd been refusing to return.'

'Yes, but remember we're talking about Ethel. Every problem has to be blamed on someone – as long as it's not Ethel. I had to remind her that Jose's AWOL career had started before I became dean, and that the initial leave had been approved by her. I also had records of all my emails asking Jose to come back. That's what saved me.'

'Of course, so it's all blown over now?'

'Far from it. My last conversation on the matter with Ethel is engraved on my memory like an unwanted tattoo. I made the mistake of saying it was good that Jose was gone and we'd saved a hundred and fifty grand off the salary budget. You know what she said?'

'She wasn't grateful?'

'She wasn't. Her comment was, "We were lucky, no thanks to you. This year I'm going to send a list of all staff members to their heads of units, who will confirm to me in writing that they've held annual progress meetings. Don't let this ever happen again. You embarrassed me in front of the Acting Vice-Chancellor. He doesn't suffer fools gladly and neither do I."'

'That's the Ethel Doctrine: it's always someone else's fault.'

'It is. Anyway, that's where things stand between Ethel and me. I've seen how she's wrecked other people's lives, but I thought I was immune. What an idiot. No one's immune to Ethel.'

***

Medway returned to the deanery for his 4 pm supervision. This was with Harriet Credopol, a precious young woman who was writing a PhD thesis on the French poststructualist, Michel Foucault. The work was supervised jointly by Medway and old Florence Lugg-Vesty from Sociology. Harriet's basic argument was that Foucault was a beacon of liberation from the hegemonic discourse of liberal democracy. Medway was not ideally qualified to supervise this work but had agreed because no one else was available. In his view Foucault was an especially loathsome carrier of the plague of postmodernism, or 'pomo', that was now widespread in the academy. In the US it was omnipresent, and Medway had suffered through many lectures and seminars where various things had been 'deconstructed', 'unmasked', and 'decentred.' The School did have a few outright postmodernists on its staff, but they were all busy with other things, and Harriet had to make do with Medway and Florence.

Medway was no expert, but he had read and heard enough to know that, according to pomo, the concept of 'truth' was now suspect, and that no particular claim to truth should be privileged over any other. In particular, 'metanarratives', or epic stories embodying some set of truth-claims – such as

Biblical redemption, or the liberal story of progress, or the Marxist prediction of proletarian revolution – were all highly suspect. As part of this view, exponents of pomo believed that there should be no substantial theory of 'the subject', or the best sort of person to be, whether Christian or liberal or Marxist or whatever. 'The other' must always be respected.

This general position came in two varieties. The first wore a smiley face and delighted in the thought that if no view was more true than any other, then all voices were equal and restrictive ideas about how to live could be cast aside. These included the principles of liberal democracy, which were alleged to be just as limiting as any other. This cheerful kind of pomo promised liberation. The second version, associated with Foucault, wore more of a sourpuss expression, and asserted that ideas about how to live were not only unjustified by any solid foundation but were also, ultimately, systems by which some people exercised power over others. Basically, all norms were tyrannical because they were expressions of power. All subjects were enmeshed in a network of power, and only local, 'micro' resistance was possible.

Harriet retailed the sourpuss, Foucauldian version, with which she obviously sympathised, and about which she raised no questions. This absence of a critical dimension was something that Medway felt obliged to point out.

'Harriet,' he said when they met in the deanery, 'you've done a lot of work and clearly know your Foucault. However, I think there are one or two issues you might want to take into account.'

'Yes, what are they?' replied Harriet suspiciously.

'Well, one is that if all voices are equally legitimate, doesn't that include sexist, racist and fascist voices? And if you have to accept them as legitimate, then how do you prevent them from oppressing those they regard as inferior or disposable?'

'Obviously,' Harriet replied, scarcely repressing the kind of deep sigh usually reserved for addressing idiots, 'that's not what Foucault is saying.' Harriet always said the name 'Foucault' in what she imagined was its correct French pronunciation but with a nasal Australian intonation as if she was trying to say the name through a reed-based wind instrument. The result was a strangled sound that came out as 'Foucoo.'

'Sexist, racist and fascist voices,' she continued, 'are not legitimate on Foucoo's view, because they are not themselves respectful of the other.'

'But if you exclude those voices,' Medway replied, 'then aren't you setting up just the kind of theory of the ideal subject that postmodernism is supposed to reject? Everyone would be respected except certain sorts of people, i.e. those who hold the wrong views. What then has happened to the rejection of truth and metanarratives? It turns out that pomo – sorry, postmodernism – has a metanarrative of its own. And on your version it sounds much like the metanarrative of liberalism.'

Harriet's face hardened into a mask of indignation. 'Foucoo and other postmodernists teach us that the notion of truth is dangerous. It's always being used to oppress people, to impose on them norms that are not theirs.'

'Is it the idea of truth itself that's dangerous, or particular versions of the truth? The purported truth of sexists, racists and fascists is oppressive, yes, but does that show that the notion of truth itself should be abandoned? In fact, as I've just suggested, aren't you proposing a truth of your own when you agree with me in condemning those voices? They should be condemned in part because they're pedlars of falsity.'

'No,' Harriet returned, 'their views should be resisted because they amount to the use of power to oppress other people. Foucoo is all about power. Norms are just power. The values of well-meaning liberals like you are just another expression of power.'

'Yes, but according to Foucoo – I mean, Foucault – the norms *you* favour must also be an expression of power. So, what's to choose between your power and my power or the power of the fascist? What's the difference between good power and bad power? Good and bad are norms, and Foucault says norms are just power. So, how does he discriminate between the kind of power that should be embraced and the kind that should be resisted?'

'Well, it's just obvious,' said Harriet, looking increasingly flushed.

'Is it?' Medway replied. 'It would be obvious enough to a liberal, because liberals can refer to values such as liberty and equality. Where these are denied, power has gone too far. But how can power ever go too far on Foucault's view, since he says that power is all there really is?'

Harriet fixed Medway with a hurt, angry look but said nothing.

'Let's take an example,' said Medway, suddenly inspired. 'Suppose the University decides to impose a new Vice-Chancellor on us who's completely inappropriate. How would we argue against that on the basis of Foucault?'

'We'd say they're just using their power to normalise us in accordance with their metanarrative,' said Harriet.

'Right. But then, can't the University say the same thing to us? They can say that we're trying to normalise the University in accordance with *our* metanarrative. If there are no ethical standards outside of power relations, then there's no basis from which to judge that one side is any better than the other. How can you speak truth to power if truth *is* power?'

Harriet was silent.

'And another thing,' Medway added, warming to his theme but oblivious to the warning signs telegraphed by Harriet. 'If the postmodernists are correct, and all voices are equal, then their own position is no more legitimate than that of the people they're arguing with – the Christians, liberals, Marxists, etc. Those other views have no unique claim to the truth, but then neither do the postmodernists. So, what are they saying? Aren't they in fact contradicting themselves: on the one hand saying there's no truth, on the other saying their view is true? Or, if they're not saying that, then are they just putting forward their view as one among others? But in that case, they must be saying in effect that the alternatives are just as legitimate. So, in the end, isn't their whole position a complete shambles?'

Harriet stood up and began gathering her things. 'I don't think these questions are fair,' she said, her voice trembling.

'Harriet, I'm only trying to raise the kind of issues I think your examiners will bring up. It's only fair to raise these questions now so you can respond to them.'

'I'd expected you to be more supportive,' sobbed Harriet, now in full flood. 'Florence doesn't treat me like this. She said my draft was great.'

Well, that's Florence for you, thought Medway. In Medway's view, Florence specialised in striking radical postures but had little capacity for critical analysis. However, he managed to restrain himself from saying this.

'I'm sure Florence has her view,' he managed to say, 'but I can only say what I think.' But Harriet was gone.

Looking back on this, Medway could see that he was in the wrong. He still thought that Foucault was deeply and fatally mistaken, and would not be much help in the debate about Murdo. But that was probably not a point he should have been pressing here. The fact was that Foucault had influenced, indeed persuaded, so many people of his nonsense, which seemed, somehow, to coalesce with the mood of the times, that he had given birth to a whole literature. To position oneself in that literature had become perfectly acceptable, no matter how erroneous the premises of the whole enterprise may be. It's as if the belief that the moon is made of green cheese has become accepted by a very large and influential group of scholars. Astronomers and astrophysicists may disagree with them, indeed may be able to demonstrate scientifically that the green-cheese belief is false. The green-cheese scholars are not interested in those contrary opinions or proofs and persist in their shared theory, which shows that the scientists are just pursuing their own power-trip. Moreover, there are enough green-cheese adherents to generate a large internal conversation – about the shade of green involved, the kind of cheese and so forth – and their theory is romantically attractive enough to draw in further generations of green-cheese acolytes. In that context it's probably a mistake to bother people like Harriet with annoying questions about first principles. If so, perhaps Florence was right after all to let her proceed unimpeded with the question of whether the verdant lunar surface is made of cheddar or Jarlsberg.

6

SOCIAL WORK

As he'd promised, Medway wrote to Goldfinger on behalf of the School, asking for an interview so he could express their concerns about Murdo's appointment. As he'd expected, Goldfinger noted his comments but declined to see him, since the decision had already been made. It would be some weeks before Murdo arrived to take up his position, but he was on his way. Also as Medway had expected, Ethel didn't like his message to the Chancellor, since it subverted the proper reporting hierarchy – Medway, as a mere school dean should have reported to Ethel first, who would decide about any approach to the higher-ups. She made her displeasure clear with a private dressing-down followed by some barbed remarks and intense squinting.

But Medway was now occupied by other matters. His fingers danced over the keyboard; he was in full flow. Was it a new book he was working on? Perhaps a lecture or a conference presentation? No, it was a 'business case' for a temporary, part-time staff appointment in the Social Work department. The need for this kind of exercise had begun when a budget shortfall was 'discovered' by the University's central administration. Exactly why this hole had appeared was not explained but perhaps it was like the case some years earlier when someone in the central finance unit had diverted two million dollars of the University's money to his favourite football team. At any rate, the shortfall led immediately to a general freeze on hiring. In the face of rising student numbers in fields such as social work, this was not good news for the School. Medway could still apply for exemptions to the freeze, but these had to be backed by an argument that demonstrated how the proposed appointment would generate more income for the University.

One area where there seemed to be no shortage of money, however, was infrastructure. Among several building projects the university was pursuing, the refurbishment and redesign of Hayek South was the one that affected Medway and his colleagues most immediately. In the year before Medway became dean, the School had to move out of the building while the reconstruction was going on. It relocated to temporary quarters further up the tree of knowledge, among the jars, gasses, rats and mice of the natural sciences – a deeply disorienting experience, since the members of the School had been accustomed to regard the upper branches of the tree as another country, where people did things differently. For their part, the natural scientists saw the social scientists suddenly in their midst in the way the country gentry saw the child evacuees from London in the Second World

War: ragged refugees from unfortunate backgrounds with doubtful hygiene.

By the time Medway assumed office, the work had been completed and they had returned to their freshly upgraded territory. Some things had not changed much. The airconditioning system, for example, retained its traditional character, impervious to the wishes of most of the building's occupants. But there were changes too. The sealing off of the Labyrinth and Bunker has been mentioned already. Another change was smaller but still significant: the individual staff offices no longer contained a reading chair. In the old office-studies there always had been a 1970s-style easy chair with a wooden frame and removable rubbery sections covered in some unnameable brown material. These chairs were not pretty but did the job for those wishing to sit comfortably to read things such as books. They were now gone, replaced by uniform circular meeting tables with matching chairs, all in off-white plastic. There was a cultural message here: no one should be reading books for any extended period; staff should be either working at their terminals or having meetings.

***

Seated at his terminal, Medway was expecting a visit from Nola 'the Flamingo' Corrigan, the monopedal head of Social Work. Medway was fond of Nola and carefully cleared a channel free of furniture so she could hop easily from the door to a chair at his conference table.

The Social Work department was a constant worry to Medway. When he started as dean, he knew nothing about social work, but he soon came to learn that it was a complex world. The social workers took up more of his time than all the other three school disciplines put together. In his mind, throughout this period, there ran a constant refrain:

> But at my back I always hear
> Social workers hurrying near.

The discipline Nola presided over was a seething cauldron of anguish and conflict. Before Medway met them, his general image of social workers was of well-meaning, politically correct professionals whose business is to make sure everyone is treated with maximum concern and respect. He was aware of the low opinion in which they were held by Rumpole of the Bailey, but was prepared to give them the benefit of the doubt. However, it turned out that the School's social workers had little in common with Medway's ideal and that Rumpole was closer to the truth. The social workers were constantly at war: with the University, with the Faculty, and with each other.

Of course, there is always a good deal of conflict in academic life, but in the field of conflict the social workers seemed to outdo every other group of academics Medway had known. Why was this? According to one theory, social workers were social workers because they themselves needed social workers. They were motivated to join the profession because they suffered from various wounds, traumas and disadvantages that (they believed) only the skills of social workers could set right. They were trying to self-medicate. But the skills they acquired as social work professionals were only a veneer. Deep down – maybe not so deep down – they were still driven by their original wounds, traumas and disadvantages. For Medway, the theory remained an interesting speculation. What was certainly true was that his social workers were permanently embattled on a number of fronts.

For a start, Nola and her supporters had one view of how the discipline should be run, but there was an opposing faction grouped around an elderly associate professor, Charlotte Pensky, who had different ideas. Things were made more difficult by the fact that Pensky seemed to have an inside line to Ethel, who favoured her way of seeing things and was happy to help Pensky undermine Nola wherever possible.

There were also occasional tensions between the academic lecturers and the Field Education ('Field Ed') unit within the discipline, which was responsible for the massive program of 'placements.' Placements were practical exercises that all social work students had to complete successfully if they wanted to qualify as professionals in the field. The students would be inserted into an institutional setting – a school, say – for a semester, and given experience of what social work would be like in practice. The Field Ed team were constantly under pressure to find placements for hundreds of students, and then to monitor the progress of those students.

If Social Work as a whole was a distinctive world, Field Ed was a world within a world. They had their own manager, who was fiercely protective of their unique interests. They held their own special meetings which, like those of a religious sect, always began with a kind of prayer combining an indigenous 'welcome to country' with a sort of pledge of allegiance to the common cause of social justice. Medway later seemed to remember them holding hands while they were doing this, but he wondered if that was his own retrospective invention, conditioned by the general missionary-like atmosphere. In the Leichardt organisation Field Ed were classed as administrators, not academics. But all the formal academic work of the students, including the written exercises connected with placements, had to be marked by the Social Work academics. So, there was rich potential for demarcation disputes between the two groups.

In addition, Social Work was no different from other units in its potential for generating personal conflicts. One lecturer, in particular, a Greek academic called Panos, seemed to offend and outrage almost everyone else. Medway liked him personally, but Panos was a vigorous proponent of a Freudian approach to social work that was regarded by most of his colleagues as on a level with the medieval theory of the humours, or voodoo, or perhaps even trickle-down economics. In view of the general set against him, it was a puzzle to Medway how he had been appointed in the first place. On his side, Panos had little time for his colleagues, whom he regarded as shallow idiots, unwilling to face up to the role of the unconscious in social (or unsocial) behaviour.

Indeed, Panos was apt to be critical of many people, referring cheerfully to his compatriots as 'fucking Greeks.' By mutual consent, he eventually moved his office to another building, away from the rest of Social Work.

But the worst conflicts were between Social Work on one side and the Faculty (i.e. Ethel) and University on the other. The fundamental problem was that the Faculty and University had discovered that Social Work was a remarkably productive cash cow. Floods of international students applied to take the Master of Social Work degree, and they were all full fee-paying – as opposed to the local students, who were partially (though inadequately) subsidised by the government. The paying of full fees made the international students the most desirable students of all. So, every year the number of applicants increased: 400 one year, 500 the next, then 600. It was the largest social work course in the country.

Why so many people wanted to do the social work Masters was an interesting question. According to the social workers, it often had little to do with social work. When they interviewed the students, mostly from China or India, they discovered that their new charges often had little idea of what social work was, and sometimes little interest in finding out. One Chinese student expressed surprise and disappointment that the field seemed to involve so much contact with members of the public. There was a strong suspicion that the Master of Social Work, an accredited professional qualification, was simply a way of obtaining permanent employment and residence in Australia.

The increasing numbers would have been less of a problem if the Faculty and University had been willing to increase Social Work's resources proportionally. However, the Faculty and University were not willing to do this. It was a source of delight to Ethel and her masters that more and more income could be extracted from Social Work with much the same expenditure. The lecturers could simply teach more students, and Field Ed could find more placements. Obviously, this put increasing pressure on the staff involved, but that was a price that senior management was willing to pay.

Nor were the problems wholly about resources. Ethel liked to boast about the Master of Social Work being the largest and therefore most popular course of its kind in Australia. A large part of the reason why it was so popular was that it was relatively easy to get into. There was an English language proficiency requirement, but this was set at a very modest level. Some of the students, when they arrived, turned out to have a reasonable standard of English; others could hardly understand, let alone speak, a word. Questions were raised about whether it was entirely desirable for people charged with the welfare of children, for example, to be unable to communicate adequately in English. Crash courses in English were instituted for the worst cases, but these took time and resources away from the teaching of the degree itself.

The upshot was that, at the start of every semester, the Social Work corridors were pervaded by a fresh sense of crisis and panic when the new, invariably increased enrolment numbers were announced for the Master of Social Work. Lecturers despaired of handling their enormous classes without any further help with tutoring and marking, and Field Ed was frantic at the prospect of trying to find an extra hundred placements beyond those they had only just managed to unearth last time.

'Geoff, we have to do something about this,' said Nola, now settled at the conference table. 'Would you be willing to come with me to meet with Ethel and make a proposal? We want to suggest a cap on enrolment numbers for the Masters. Even a temporary cap might allow us some breathing space to regroup and cope better in future.'

'Of course,' said Medway. 'I'll ask Astrid to set up the meeting.'

The meeting did not take place in the Bunker, or even the Wolf's Lair, but in an alternative location in the Nozick Building, at the very apex of the tree of knowledge adjacent to the Ultima Thule carpark. Nervous breakdowns having become almost mandatory for Ethel's school deans, the dean of Business, Professor Pinfold, achieved his collapse after only a few months in the job, shortly after one of his weekly meetings with Ethel. Ethel had attributed Pinfold's departure to his wife's being unhappy, but she had probably been unhappy because her husband was now clucking like a chicken. Ethel decided to take over the Business School herself and was now spending a lot of time in the School's office up on the third floor of the Nozick Building, a location Medway thought of as 'the Eagle's Nest.' This was where the meeting with Medway and Nola would take place. Usually they would go up there together but Nola had an appointment just beforehand, so they agreed to make their way separately.

After a steep climb, Medway reached the Eagle's Nest slightly early and was greeted by Ethel's minder, Doris. As a Vice President and Executive Dean, Ethel rated not just a PA but an EA – an executive assistant – and Doris occupied this exalted station. She was an elderly woman who walked like a sailor and possessed all the charm and delicacy of Saddam Hussein. Medway suspected that in her free time she smoked a pipe, or maybe just chewed tobacco.

Nola had not yet arrived but Medway was immediately ushered into the lair, where Ethel was waiting.

'Sorry, Geoff,' she said, 'there's no possibility of a cap on these numbers. This is a wonderfully popular course, and an obvious area for us to expand. It makes money, and we need the income.'

'In that case,' replied Medway, 'would you be willing to give us more resources to teach these additional numbers?'

'I can't see why. You have adequate resources already.'

'But you realise, Ethel, that some of these students – the international students in particular – are so ill-prepared for study at Masters level in Australia. Their language skills, in particular, are often appalling.'

'Well, it's your job to fix that. Frankly, it disappoints me that you hate your students.' Vintage Ethel: the old magician's device of misdirection once again, as in the Bodkin case. Disorient the opposition by throwing in an irrelevant and preferably outrageous accusation that will distract attention from the real issue. Medway recalled Nick telling him about an expression now popular in political circles: 'throwing a dead cat on the table.' Ethel could hurl any number of cats. Medway was tempted to go in for some feline tossing of his own: I'm disappointed you hate your staff, he was on the brink of saying. Instead, he said,

'For heaven's sake, Ethel, I don't hate my students. I'm just trying to be realistic about what's needed to teach them.'

'You hate them, and you shouldn't. You mustn't give up on students. I myself was categorised as a hopeless failure in my early years at university. I had to battle for years to overcome that.' Interesting, thought Medway. Whoever it was who had condemned Ethel's fledgling efforts had called down her wrath on everyone who followed. She was still angry, and still angrily trying to assert her limited abilities. Anyone who disagreed with her echoed, in her mind, the contempt of those early teachers, and became not only opponents but enemies, wilful obstacles to her mission of self-justification.

Beginning to frighten himself with this line of thought, Medway looked around for the reassuring presence of Nola. Her support would have been useful at this point, but where was she? There was a knock on the door and the Popeye features of Doris intruded into the room.

'Sorry to interrupt you, Ethel, but I've had a call from Nola. The lift is out of order, and she can't get up the stairs.' Sometimes, having one leg can be a real nuisance. Medway could imagine Nola fuming below, like Long John Silver without the parrot.

While the politically correct might try to accommodate disabilities or other special circumstances, Ethel would generally make no such sentimental allowances – unless, perhaps, someone was watching who had authority greater than her own, like a Vice-Chancellor. There was even less accommodation in the case of people, like Nola, who irritated or challenged her. Indeed, such cases gave Ethel an opportunity to indulge her playful sadism.

'Tell her not to bother,' she said with a studied callousness, enjoying the moment.

'But Ethel,' Medway spluttered, 'you could at least hear what she has to say. I can give you the general picture, but Nola has all the details. This is all about the conditions actually being experienced by the staff.'

'I don't need to be told what the conditions are. I know what they are. You're both wasting my time.' Ethel turned away towards her computer screen, the customary signal that her interlocutor was dismissed.

For a moment Medway wondered if it might be possible to take advantage of the third-floor location and defenestrate Ethel. He'd had similar thoughts after the Bodkin interview but these were frustrated because the Bunker was on the ground floor. The Eagle's Nest was a different matter. Down below was the unyielding surface of the Ultima Thule carpark and the thought of Ethel flying through the air to her doom was appealing – perhaps her impact would be registered by one of the domed parking sensors. The practical difficulty would be to wrestle her bulk through the small window – it would be like wrangling an inflated airbag – before Doris intervened. Deciding it was too hard this time, he packed up and left, filing the idea away for further reflection.

In the weeks that followed, the social workers received some unexpected support from an external source, and for a while this gave them hope. The CEO of the state Social Access Network (SANE) wrote to the Acting Vice-Chancellor, Roy Beadle, raising concerns about Leichardt's Field Ed placements. The letter complained about the pressure on agencies to place unsustainable numbers of students, and about the number of international students from Leichardt who had neither the language nor the cultural background necessary for them to function adequately in their placement. Basically, Leichardt's social work students were like a plague of locusts who were devouring the crops and leaving nothing of value in return. This was a serious matter because SANE was the accrediting agency for Leichardt's Master of Social Work degree. That degree would cease to be worth anything professionally if its accreditation was withdrawn.

Beadle invited Nola to come and see him directly, and Nola arranged for Medway to be invited too. This seemed to be progress, because for once the conversation would circumvent Ethel. The question often occurred to Medway whether Ethel's stonewalling of everything to do with income and resources was her own doing or whether she was just doing the bidding of her own masters higher up in the management of the University. The meeting with Beadle would be an interesting test.

Nola and Medway presented themselves at Beadle's office with a degree of optimism. They were greeted affably by Beadle, a tall, stooping, shambling figure with prominent dark bags under his eyes and a rapidly developing paunch. Beadle offered them coffee and proceeded to crush their optimism into a fine powder.

'Accreditation agencies are always pushing their weight around like this, and Leichardt will not be pushed around,' said Beadle, speaking up bravely for the Leichardt David against the SANE Goliath. 'The Master of Social Work program provides an important stream of revenue for the University, and we will not be doing anything that will reduce that revenue. We will continue to expand the program, and that means Field Ed will continue to find the necessary placements.'

Nola and Medway tried to get Beadle to listen, but to no avail. He didn't seem altogether comfortable, but his attitude was chiselled in concrete: SANE were the aggressors, trying to bully the innocent University and to deter it from its legitimate quest for money. So, the problem was not just Ethel; she was, to some extent at least, the cat's-paw of the University. Once again, the bottom line was cash, and nothing would divert the University from its pursuit.

7

TARGET 1%

At last, the following semester, Murdo arrived on campus. His inaugural speech was timed to coincide with the grand opening of the University's redesigned Company Headquarters (CHQ), the town square at the centre of the administrative and service buildings that had been known as the Res Publica when Medway first came to Leichardt. The relaunch of CHQ was a splendid occasion. Guided by his minders to a podium, Murdo looked out over a vast throng of students and staff, all waiting, open-mouthed with excitement, for him to begin. It reminded him of taking guard in a test match, and his breast swelled with pride at the prospect of the coming adulation.

CHQ was impressive. The first thing Murdo noticed was that his podium was positioned in front of a statue which depicted a man in what looked like pioneer clobber staring out into the distance. The bloke who'd been in charge of Murdo's introductory briefing, Roy Beadle, told him that this was a statue of the explorer Leichhardt, after whom the

University had been named – or misnamed, apparently, since Beadle said they'd accidentally turned Leichhardt into Leichardt. Murdo couldn't help wondering how successful this Leichhardt/Leichardt had been as an explorer, since he'd vanished without trace – at least, that's what Beadle said; Murdo had never heard of the guy. Beadle also said that having the statue in the background – by the way, it featured, in addition, the explorer's faithful dog, a mongrel called Perdy – would 'add legitimacy' to Murdo's speech. Murdo wasn't quite sure what this meant but took from it the general idea that the presence of this failed explorer and his pooch would somehow class up what Murdo had to say. Well, whatever.

CHQ was framed by the university's main public buildings. Facing Murdo, at the top of the amphitheatre, was the Adam Smith Communications Hub (in the old days the Webb Library). On the northern side, the Milton Friedman (formerly Chifley) Building contained the Council Room and offices of the middle and lower levels of administration. Opposite that, running along the southern margin of the amphitheatre, was the Client Services Centre (previously the Student Union Building). At Murdo's back, just behind the statue of the explorer, a brand-new office-block had been constructed to house the Vice-Chancellor and his staff, of which more in a moment.

CHQ was being relaunched because, Beadle said, it had been radically redesigned. Apparently, on the spot where the new office-block now stood, the old CHQ had boasted a lawn with a concrete stage in the middle where bands played and rabble-rousers incited crowds of students to foment revolution. In the new design, that whole layer had been scooped out so that, as Murdo stood facing uphill to the west, there rose in front of him a steep amphitheatre. On its terraces, students had beanbags to sit in or lie on, although it was standing room only today.

Murdo could see that the amphitheatre was a definite improvement on what had gone before. Instead of the former lawn and stage with students circulating haphazardly around it, threatening public order, now everyone sat looking ahead in the same direction. The tiered seating suggested a natural hierarchy in place of the swirling chaos that must have reigned before. Better still, where the students previously had nothing better to focus on than dreadful bands and dangerous lefties, now they had in front of them, suspended high on the building at Murdo's back, a gigantic video screen.

Facing him at the top of the amphitheatre, in front of the Adam Smith Communications Hub, Murdo could also see a large stone bust mounted on a plinth. According to Beadle, the bust depicted the ancient Greek philosopher, Aristotle. It was intended to symbolise Leichardt's profound devotion to philosophy and humane learning – apparently there was some such idea behind the amphitheatre itself – and had been donated by the local Greek community. Originally located in the dappled shade of the Humanities quad in the lower branches of the tree of knowledge, Aristotle had now been moved down to CHQ and placed at the top of the amphitheatre facing the enormous screen. Murdo smiled inwardly at the thought that this Greek clown, who had no doubt peddled a lot of nonsense and known nothing about managing a business, now had to watch daytime television for all eternity.

Looking up at the rising amphitheatre, Murdo was reminded of his favourite venue, the Melbourne Cricket Ground. The MCG was the scene of some of his greatest triumphs – like that century against the poms when they'd dropped him five times. Involuntarily, he raised his right arm in salute to the crowd, in his hand an imaginary Gray Nicholls bat – his favourite model, the 'Predator.' Well, this miniature MCG would see Murdo do just as brilliantly as he had in the past.

Certainly, some basic conditions looked to be in his favour. For one thing, the CHQ redevelopment was just one of several building projects that were coming to fruition all around the campus. In his briefing, Beadle had mentioned that the previous Vice-Chancellor, the late Professor Pound, had wisely resisted the demands of the academic staff who wanted more money for new teaching appointments and salary increases. Instead, priority was placed on infrastructure projects because these were good for public relations and marketing.

As a result, there were many infrastructural highlights: CHQ, the upgrading of Hayek South and the siting of the sensor-domes in Carpark 13 were just a few of them. In addition, there was a new Optimal Somatic Functions (health sciences) building, a Centre for Innovation, a new IT Science building, a 'senior college' for high school students specialising in STEM subjects, and an entire new campus for natural sciences and engineering constructed where a now-defunct car factory had been.

Best of all was the new office block, behind the statue of Leichhardt, that would be the headquarters of the Vice-Chancellor and senior management. The old CHQ (and Res Publica) had buildings on only three sides; the eastern edge had been fringed by the lawn with its sea view, on which the students sat, lay, slept and chased each other about. Professor Pound had spotted the lawn's untapped potential and ordered its replacement by a massive, five-storey erection of steel and glass. The view of the Pacific was obliterated by a panorama of bureaucracy.

The official name of the new structure was the Reagan-Thatcher Tower but it became known popularly as 'the Citadel.' Like Ethel's Bunker in Hayek South, the Citadel was immune to penetration from outside, access being possible only by a card-entry lift guarded by a receptionist. Murdo was amazed to hear that not everyone was happy with this development. Malcontents whispered that the senior management anticipated rough times ahead and wanted to be as secure as possible against repetitions of the great Chifley Occupation of 1970. Some old fart called Professor Toynbee, from History (appropriately), was heard to say that, in contrast with the French revolutions of the eighteenth and nineteenth centuries and with *les évènements* of '68, at Leichardt it was the authorities who were setting up the barricades. Well, let them say what they liked. Comments like that were actually quite useful to Murdo, because they showed who might need to be dropped from the team.

As well as all this building activity, Murdo registered with satisfaction the expansion of the University's senior management team in numbers, status and remuneration.

First, numbers. Back in the mists of time, Leichardt's senior management had consisted basically of three people: the Vice-Chancellor, a Deputy Vice-Chancellor (Academic), currently Roy Beadle, and a Deputy Vice-Chancellor (Research). In recent years this triumvirate had grown exponentially. First, a Deputy Vice-Chancellor (International) had been added, followed by a Deputy Vice-Chancellor (Students), then a Deputy Vice-Chancellor (Indigenous). Professor Pound had brought in two Pro-Vice-Chancellors to assist the Deputy Vice-Chancellor (Students). Each of these officials then needed their own deputies, assistants, advisers and underlings; instead of three people, there was now a vast army of executives and hangers-on. And this might yet be expanded. Murdo was interested in the suggestion made by Professor Euripides, from Law, that another executive position should be added: Groom of the Stool. He'd gone off the idea when Professor Toynbee explained what it meant, and he'd noted Euripides' name for future reference.

Second, status. The Vice-Chancellor was no longer identified as the head of some fusty outpost of the public service but as the Chief Executive Officer of a business – hence, a President as well as a Vice-Chancellor. Consequently, as noted earlier, the heads of the faculties had to be vice-presidents as well as executive deans. Then there were the new directors, nabobs and grand poobahs for various purposes. It all added up to a rich and intricate hierarchy.

Third, remuneration. Murdo would draw a salary appropriate for a CEO, the $1.2 million agreed with Goldfinger. It followed that all of his deputies and assistants, and their deputies and assistants, had to receive executive salaries proportionate to his own. Prudence Climber, the Deputy Vice-Chancellor (Students) was now driving a brand-new Porsche convertible. Of course, there was always criticism, dissent and carping, especially from the academics. Murdo had heard his management team described as 'a conga line of suck-holes,' or alternatively, 'snouts in the trough.' But you had to expect negativity from the pointy-headed brigade, and you needed to remember it was based on mere envy. If you wanted the best people, such as himself, you had to pay for them.

The critics said that all of this – the impressive infrastructure, the multiplication of executives, the grandiose executive titles and massive salaries – was evidence that the neoliberal model had triumphed. Gone was any pretence that the basic purpose of universities was to provide a public service or a liberal education, let alone to pursue knowledge for its own sake. Universities were now businesses like any other: their most fundamental purpose was to make money.

Well, on this point Murdo agreed with them. Finally, the universities, including Leichardt, were moving in the right direction.

***

A hush fell on the multitude as the new Vice-Chancellor began to speak. It was his great honour, Murdo said, to declare the new CHQ open. It would enable the University to serve ever-increasing numbers of students, including more full fee-paying international students. But more than this, it was Murdo's pleasure to announce a new agenda for the University.

'Leichardt has a lot of potential,' he said. 'But for too long it has settled for second-best. According to the rankings, we find ourselves in the top 2% of universities worldwide. But I say, why should we be satisfied with that level of mediocrity? That's not how we won the Ashes three times in a row when I captained Australia. I say, let's raise Leichardt to the top 1%! I say, let's make Leichardt great!' He had considered following the Trumpian precedent with 'Make Leichardt Great *Again*' but realised that the implication would be that Leichardt had been great at some period before Murdo's arrival. That would not make sense.

The students clapped and stamped their appreciation, thrilled by the idea of being on the winning team in some ill-defined competition. But Murdo couldn't help noticing that some of the staff members in the audience (yes, he could see them quite clearly) seemed less enthusiastic, clapping politely or not at all. He had a good memory for faces and would remember theirs.

His impression of a degree of staff resistance was confirmed in the days that followed. Sceptics were muttering that the 1% ambition was both unnecessary and absurd. It was true that being in the top 2% did not amount to much, since every genuine university in the world was in that category – the remaining 98% consisting of cowboy operations in which people could basically get degrees by mail-order. Nevertheless, the top 2% was a region of respectability containing many worthy institutions. Why would it not be enough for Leichardt to carve out a suitable niche for itself at this more modest level?

Moreover, aiming at the top 1% struck many people as plainly impossible. Like the summit of Everest, this was a rarefied realm where few had penetrated. It included places like Oxford, Cambridge, Harvard and Yale, which were backed by huge reserves of public and private funding that enabled them to buy squadrons of Nobel laureates. There wasn't the slightest chance that Leichardt could ever compete in this landscape.

There were even those who saw the 1% goal as not only out of reach but incoherent, because the whole concept of university rankings was incoherent. No single ranking could capture all of the different dimensions by which universities might be compared – publications, grants, teaching, community engagement, quality of student experience, and so on. The rankings purported to do the impossible: commensurate the incommensurable.

For Murdo, these views were just the typical mutterings of losers and defeatists. The goal of reaching the top % made sense to Murdo, and that's what counted. There had been those who said that he couldn't win three Ashes series in a row. He'd proved them wrong and would do the same with the current bunch of whiners. Sure, there would be casualties.

At a meeting when the metaphor of Everest had been brought up, that smart-arse Beadle had played with this by imagining that Murdo's path to the top would pass through a Dead Zone in which the frozen corpses of discarded staff members would be permanently on view as a warning to the noncompliant and unproductive. So, what was wrong with that? Beadle was envious because he'd wanted to be Vice-Chancellor and Murdo had edged him out. He was currently Murdo's second-in-command, but if he wasn't careful he would soon be one of the frozen corpses.

Murdo instituted a plan, which he called 'Target 1%', that promised to acquire the pot of rankings gold within five years. Details were initially lacking about how exactly this transformation would be achieved, but few had any doubt that it would involve a good deal of restructuring.

Again, there were critics. That old fool from History, Toynbee, said the idea was 'redolent of other great five-year plans, such as those of Lenin and Stalin, and Mao's Great Leap Forward. The main difference is that the Vice-Chancellor will impose the disciplines not of communism but of the market.'

Murdo didn't know what the first sentence was about, but he understood the second sentence and couldn't see the problem.

***

Murdo's agenda commenced when he sent out a survey to the staff, ostensibly consulting them about what they thought were the strengths and weaknesses of the University. According to the results released by Murdo's office, people thought that things were in general okay, except that the University suffered from too much bureaucracy. This was a predictable response, since 'too much bureaucracy' is the standard complaint of bureaucratic staff everywhere at all times. However, this was exactly what Murdo expected and wanted to hear. Those whose lives were about to be turned upside down had unwittingly given him a mandate. They had declared that Leichardt was impeded by red tape: too many levels of administration, too much duplication of official activity. Therefore, organisational change was essential.

A favourite example Murdo seized upon was a particular bureaucratic form which, he said, had to receive six different signatures before the relevant action was authorised. No one had actually seen this form or knew what it was for, but the idea of the form provided Murdo with a powerful image. In subsequent retellings of the legend, the number of required signatures grew from six signatures to eight, then ten, and eventually fourteen. At the last iteration, old Professor Tennyson, from English, muttered something about 'rogues in buckram suits.' Murdo was puzzled by the reference to 'buckram', but assumed it was some kind of new suit material and took the comment to be an obscure attack on the University's senior executives. Tennyson's name was added to the list Murdo was working on, alongside the names of Toynbee, Beadle, Euripides and others.

Murdo promised to fix this problem: he would gallop to the rescue and sweep the red tape away. The starting point was a restructuring of the administrative staff. They were at present scattered across the University, concentrated in distinct units, such as the schools and faculties, and reporting to the leaders of those units. All very irregular and inefficient. Murdo's solution was to have them report along new centralised lines of management to the grand poobahs in the Citadel. This would increase efficiency, eliminate unnecessary duplications, and enable the University to reduce administrative staff numbers (other than executives) overall. Incidentally, it would also increase the power of the University's central administration.

It was unclear how the new reporting lines would actually lead to these results (other than the last one) until a further dimension of Murdo's restructure came into view: the schools would be abolished and the faculties turned into 'colleges.' Instead of three levels of bureaucracy – university, faculties, and schools – there would now be only two – university and colleges. Two levels would surely be more efficient than three.

As usual, the doubters sang their odious songs of negativity. If the goal was to reduce three administrative layers to two, then why not abolish the faculties? (Some more radical voices advocated retaining the schools and faculties and abolishing the University.) Why the schools should go rather than the faculties was not something Murdo cared to explain, but he had a perfectly sound reason for it. The Faculty level had to be preserved because it contained some of his closest allies – namely, the executive deans he had appointed himself and whose bloated salaries depended on his patronage.

In Murdo's plan, the faculties would be retained but called colleges and their number increased from four to six. This would enable Murdo to appoint two further executive deans. Why call the faculties 'colleges'? Because they would be more 'collegiate', meaning, Murdo said, more strongly united by disciplinary affiliations than the faculties had been. Even Murdo knew this was nonsense, but his experience was that you can always get some people to believe anything, and the rest can be coerced. Divide and rule.

***

Murdo took his proposals to a forum of school deans, adding some more detail. Some schools would be swallowed whole by an appropriate college. Others would be dismembered and scattered among different colleges. By and large, the natural science schools would be kept together; it was the schools in Non-Sciences that needed more radical reorganisation. The School of Social Studies, for example, would be taken apart and redistributed among two different colleges. Politics and Public Policy, Sociology and Women's Studies would go to the new College of Non-Sciences (which was most of the old Faculty of Non-Sciences renamed as a college); Social Work would join Psychology and Criminology in a new College of Social Control. Murdo knew that the Non-Sciences people wouldn't like it, but they would make trouble anyway. His hope was that the natural scientists would take his side. He was correct on both counts.

'It seems to me,' said someone identifying himself as Medway, from Social Studies (of course!), 'that your case for the proposal has not yet been made out. I note, for a start, that you announced yesterday that Leichardt has climbed seven places in the university world rankings. If that can be achieved without this restructure, then why do we need the restructure?'

'That may have happened *in spite of* our current inefficiency,' replied the dean of Science and Engineering, radiating self-satisfaction like a Soviet reactor. 'The proposed restructure will raise our ranking further.' As I expected, thought Murdo, I can count on the scientists.

'Well, it may or it may not,' whined the mosquito Medway. 'That strikes me as speculation. The restructure will be a massive change, and its effects are unpredictable. Isn't the new ranking concrete evidence that we are getting good results without these changes?'

'But everyone knows we're being choked by bureaucracy. That's been established by the Vice-Chancellor's survey,' said the deputy dean of History, Mildred Scheisskopf, who was standing in for Professor Toynbee, absent on leave. She reminded Murdo of his first wife Tonya's mother-in-law, Doreen, a major idiot. But, unlike Doreen, Scheisskopf was clearly one of those *useful* idiots.

That couldn't be said of Professor Euripides, the dean of the Law School. 'Geoff makes a good point,' said Euripides. 'And I'd add that the proposed changes will have all kinds of ill effects that have not been considered. Take the Law School, for example. We've put a lot of effort into creating what is, in fact, the leading law school in the state and one of the best in the country. Under the proposal, it will simply disappear, and all that work with it.'

'But the discipline will still exist, won't it?' said Murdo. 'It just won't have the status of an autonomous school.'

'But that's the point,' replied Euripides. 'There won't be a "law school" anymore. Just an academic unit under the direct control of an executive dean who knows nothing about law – in more ways than one!'

'Seems like a minimal change to me,' said Murdo.

'The change will be relatively minimal in the natural sciences,' said Medway. 'All the science, health science and engineering schools will, in effect, remain intact. They'll simply be converted into disciplines within the science colleges. But my school will be split up among two different colleges. That's not such a minimal change.'

'Just an administrative rearrangement. What difference will it make?' said Murdo.

'Here's the difference. We've just spent five years making ourselves into a unitary school. The school contains four different disciplines which were thrown together, seemingly with the aid of short straws, by the last restructure we went through. We were told to turn ourselves into a unified and "vibrant" unit animated by its own shared goals – or some such waffle. And we did that. It took a lot of work. Can you imagine how it feels now to be told we can all just go back to square one?'

'Times change,' said Murdo.

'Easy for you to say,' said Euripides. 'And here's another point. Let's say we abolish the schools. The work they do still has to be done somewhere. In the end, the work of the schools will simply be reproduced within the new colleges. If it's not, how will things get done? Going back to what I said before, what does someone like Ethel Korova know about how to run a law school?'

Murdo remained unimpressed, as did his allies the dean of Science and Engineering and Mildred, the latter excited to breathlessness by her own rhetoric about 'choking.' Moreover, their view was clearly in the majority. Most of the deans thought that Murdo's plan was brilliant, a foolproof blueprint for Leichardt's future acceleration up the rankings. Certainly, the scientists were solidly behind it. Their operations would not be disrupted much. They might lose a few supernumerary admin staff, that was all.

'Okay, that's stumps,' said Murdo, happy with the way the meeting had gone. Back in the Citadel, he took out his list of names, at the top of which he'd drawn a crude skull and cross-bones, and added Medway to it.

***

Further consultations took place all over the University, Murdo delighting in bringing his gospel to ever more obscure nooks and crannies. These eventually included the School of Social Studies. He arrived at Medway's deanery accompanied by Ethel, who had told Medway earlier that she 'wouldn't miss this for the world.' Unsmiling and instinct with menace,

Murdo was clad in contemporary business chic: a grey suit with a jacket seemingly two sizes too small, white shirt with no tie, and Italian slip-on loafers. A minder wore a similar outfit, making him look like a mini-Murdo. In the deanery, Murdo chatted amiably with Ethel about key performance indicators, largely ignoring Medway until it was time for him to take them to the meeting.

Murdo was delighted to find the meeting room packed, except, oddly, for the front row, where a single academic sat on his own. As soon as Murdo entered the room, this person, who had the appearance and manner of one of the more self-important hobbits, stood up and raced over, excitedly shaking Murdo's hand and introducing himself as Bruno Whelper. Whelper seemed to think that Murdo should already know of him as some kind of media celebrity. That was news to Murdo, although Whelper's voice did remind him of Channel Nine's cartoon Daffy the Duck, who used to walk sadly across the screen, lamenting his fate, whenever anyone was out without scoring. The look of frank adoration on Whelper's face was pleasing and creepy at the same time.

The meeting began. Welcomed officially by Medway, Murdo responded by giving his standard Target 1% speech, commending the basic outlines of his master-plan, noting that its high ambitions and elevated values echoed those of the great test cricket teams of his era, and looking forward to the University's arrival on the sunlit uplands that it was bound to attain once everyone accepted and implemented the plan.

A Q and A period followed, featuring contributions from Medway and three women, who introduced themselves as, respectively, Nola Corrigan, the head of Social Work (who seemed to be lacking a leg – could that be right?), Kate Cardigan, from Public Policy (one of those spinster-types although more than a bit forbidding), and Millicent Something-Something, an incredibly loud woman from Women's Studies (is that a subject?). Murdo scribbled down their names in his notebook – although he was told later that the Cardigan woman was some kind of elite professor who couldn't be touched.

They all asked the same basic question: why was it such a great idea to dismantle the School when it had done so well? According to the University's own data, the School consistently achieved a financial surplus (a rare feat for any school in Leichardt), excellent student demand, and strong research performance. It was extremely disappointing to see in the proposed college structure the scattering of the School to the winds. The 'synergies' (a favourite word in Murdo's jargon) among the School's disciplines would be lost and the hard work put into making the School operate effectively would be wasted. All this would be highly disruptive and the School saw it as a poor reward for its efforts and achievements over the six years of its existence. Against this cost, little was to be gained by the move, which was unlikely to achieve its stated goal of reducing hierarchy and bureaucracy.

Murdo had little interest in any of this. He made no eye-contact with any of the questioners, looking down at the table in front of him and fiddling with a paper-clip. At one point he picked up a ruler and seemed to be practising his forward defence. His eyes bulged and rolled slightly at mentions of the School's achievements.

Eventually, the desperate puffing concluded and Murdo was able to respond.

'It's true,' he said, barely stifling a yawn, 'that this school' – he couldn't for the moment recall its name, but no matter – 'has done passably well according to some key performance indicators. But in others it lags behind.'

Chests that had inflated with pride at the recitation of the School's achievements now sagged like punctured beachballs.

'In particular,' Murdo continued, 'while your publication record isn't bad' – here Murdo pulled a face to signal that he was generously conceding a point that he really shouldn't – 'your performance in terms of external grant funding is far below expected levels.'

Murdo went on ruthlessly to expose the School's shortcomings when it came to obtaining grants. Other achievements counted for little beside this. It was plain that the self-image of Medway and his colleagues as a successful School was not shared by the Vice-Chancellor. As far as he was concerned, they were wastes of space, more or less on a par with the England cricket teams he'd known.

He finished with a warning, clothed not so much in a veil as in a piece of transparent cling-wrap. 'Of course, there may be some who see things differently,' he said, his convex eyes, like swivelling surveillance cameras, seeking out those who had defended the School. If he had been speaking entirely in his own voice he would then have referred simply to those people who were no longer willing to be part of that sacred body, the team. But he decided that the intellectuals of Leichardt would be more impressed by a phrase that Roy Beadle had come up with: 'Those whose aspirations no longer align with those of the University are, of course, free to go elsewhere.' It was a phrase that came to serve Murdo well over the coming weeks.

8

GREAT EXPECTATIONS

'Geoffrey, don't forget the tree surgeon's coming at 9 am.'

It was Thursday, Medway's 'research day', when he worked at home. He needed to make the most of this precious time, and he could do without these interruptions. But Sarah had asked him to help her interview the tree surgeon, who was coming to give a quote for pruning the large Chinese elm at the back of the house.

'Okay, I won't forget.'

'I see the people down the road have found a solution to managing their elephant grass,' said Sarah.

'What's their solution?' asked Medway.

'They have a bobcat working in there, taking out the whole lawn. They're obviously going to concrete over the whole thing. Why buy a house in the suburbs if you're not prepared to maintain the garden properly?'

Sarah was, herself, a dedicated and hard-working gardener who spent hours outside, meticulously clipping, trimming, digging, planting, pruning and picking up tiny pieces of debris. She did it all herself, asking Medway only to mow the lawns and occasionally to carry heavy things like the larger plant-pots and bags of manure. She regarded all this labour as simply what one did and couldn't understand people who didn't think the same.

'Of course, it's typical of this area. No-one gives a toss about their gardens, so we have to live surrounded by pigsties,' said Sarah.

'Yes, it's disappointing, but what can you do? Other people have different priorities,' said Medway, immediately regretting this comment.

'It's all very well for you in your hut. I'm out in the garden all the time having to cope with it all. But you're right about priorities. The priority of the weirdo next door is to be somewhere else, so his abandoned hovel is an overgrown haven for possums, mice and God knows what. The priority of Snibbo and Bibbo on the other side is to live in a nuclear bomb-proof bunker surrounded by a "native" garden that looks like a piece of scrubland.' Snibbo and Bibbo (not their real names) were an elderly couple who frequently irritated Sarah when their gigantic Queensland Box dropped its junk over the driveway. The two ancients would then use a blower-vac to relocate the mess to the street, where it would either clog up the gutters or blow back again. The cry, 'Snibbo's out with the blower-vac again!', was a standing joke in the Medway household.

'And then there's the Psychologist,' Sarah continued, 'whose pigsty is even worse than the Weirdo's. Columns of rats scurry along the top of his fence all night long. You can see their eyes reflected in the lights. What did we do to deserve these people!'

There was a knock on the front door. The tree surgeon was about 15 minutes early. In Medway's experience, the usual pattern with tradies was that they either kept you waiting for hours or didn't show at all, but occasionally they appeared ahead of time just to keep you on your toes. This one turned out to be tall and athletic, with gingery hair, an orangey tan, and a reassuringly honest, open look about him. He seemed oddly familiar but Medway couldn't place him. His name was Phil.

The interview went well. Sarah explained what she thought needed doing, and Phil agreed that it all made sense and he could do it 'no worries.' There was also, as usual in such cases, a brief period when Sarah got off the point a bit, rehearsing for Phil her theme of the oppression she experienced because of the surrounding hovels. Her flow was disrupted somewhat when Phil asked, 'What's a "hovel"?' But he concluded that the job would be no problem and he'd send his quote the following day.

***

Even in his hut, Medway still had trouble getting started. It was ever thus. After two or three days on his teaching and admin duties, shifting his mind into the research realm was like trying to become a different person. Today, in addition, he was haunted by what he had heard from the new Vice-Chancellor.

He did manage to turn his computer on and read and reply to his emails. He'd meant to set aside half an hour for this, but the half-hour turned into an hour. Then he got up to do some stretching. After that, he decided to make another coffee. Should he have a biscuit? No, but what the hell. Twenty minutes later he got up again to go to the toilet. On his way back he popped into the spare room to examine some books that, much to Sarah's disgust, he had stored there. After that it was time for lunch, and he had done virtually nothing.

Post-lunch he had a brief power-nap and, somewhat refreshed, was able to focus by promising himself that he need only work for an hour before having another break. Thus cleverly outflanking his inertia, he began by reviewing the overall position.

His publications, in abeyance while he was learning the dean ropes, had begun to get back on track with a new book project. It had taken a while to find a publisher. His last publisher, Polity, said his project was 'too academic and not commercial enough', and recommended Oxford University Press. OUP responded that the project was too commercial and not academic enough, and recommended Polity. But eventually he found a home for it. The proposal was reviewed and approved, a contract signed. He was back in business.

There was a shadow, however: he had no grants.

When Medway had arrived at Leichardt, back in the relative innocence of the previous century, research and publication had been regarded in the Politics department as hobbies pursued only by the pretentious. Those attempting to publish were scornfully described as 'soaring with the eagles.' The workload plan, which supposedly assigned work equally, did not recognise research at all.

But then, as government funding dried up, the University realised that it could increase its share of what was left by raising its publication game. At first it encouraged sheer numbers of publications, later it became more concerned with 'quality' as measured by journal and publisher rankings. Now, not even high-quality publications were enough. The new game was the winning of research grants from sources external to the University. Once the funding was secured, it scarcely mattered to the University what was done with it – except that some sort of publication outcome was usually thought to be necessary in order to establish a track record that would support the next grant. The vital goal was getting the money.

Medway had rarely pursued external grants because they were unnecessary for his research. Unlike his counterparts in the natural sciences, he did not need laboratories, equipment and research assistants. What he needed was time and autonomy – or academic independence, as it used to be called. These were his chief tools – along with the books – pitifully old-fashioned as they now seemed. But the getting of competitive research money, regardless of whether it was actually needed for research, and irrespective of whether anything worthwhile was being done with it, had become a fetish. This had been confirmed for Medway earlier in the week when Murdo had visited the School to 'consult' them about Target 1%.

Worse was to come. A week after Murdo's visit to the School, the University brought in a new system of 'research performance expectations.' Its key feature was that everyone was expected to win a minimum amount of grant money from sources outside the University. The origin of this was said to be the federal government's recently revised formula for calculating universities' public research funding, which was based entirely on the level of funding they managed to secure for themselves through competitive grants.

Hence arose the idea that Leichardt would expect everyone to meet a minimum external grant target. The proposal had been under review for months. When the schools were consulted about their responses (since each school was given its own targets), Medway had suggested limits that reflected something like the modest amounts most people actually succeeded in winning. He knew this would not be accepted but felt he had to choose between being shot in the head by the University and shooting himself. He decided not to do their job for them.

He was working late one night when he received a call from Ethel summoning him to the Bunker.

'I've reviewed your proposed grant targets, Geoff, and they're far too small,' said Ethel, as if pointing out that Medway was wearing odd socks.

'Really? I entered numbers that seemed realistic.'

'Your numbers can't be realistic. I've got the figures here for average grant income per academic for the last five years. Here, have a look at this.'

Medway saw a set of numbers that made him feel ill. They might be possible for someone like Professor Cardigan, but for most people, including himself, they were so far out of reach as to seem like messages from another universe.

'These,' Ethel continued, 'are no more than the amounts everyone is already averaging right now. So, these should be your targets.'

Medway marvelled at Ethel's facile reasoning. He knew she would not be interested but tried anyway.

'Ethel, this "average" amount of grant money that everyone is supposed to receive is a fiction. No one receives an average amount of grant money. In a system of competitive grants the winner takes it all – or a few winners – no one else gets anything. The winners are always a minority; if that weren't the case, it wouldn't be a competition. Nor can there be any expectation that if you missed out in one year you'd succeed in another. Each time, there are winners and losers, and everyone is a loser except the few lucky winners.'

'I don't know what you're talking about. These are the figures. The Vice-Chancellor isn't interested in sob-stories from losers. It's true, you do need to *win* a competitive grant. So, you and your fellow-losers had better get on and do that.' Ethel turned back to her computer and Medway was dismissed.

When the final targets were released, they were, of course, the same eye-watering figures Medway had seen in the

Bunker. It was clear that he, for one, would be unable to satisfy them. The prospects for getting a grant for a political-theory project were extremely remote. He went along to an information session where he was told that 80% of the Australian Research Council's grants were reserved, in accordance with official government priorities, for the natural sciences. The remaining 20% were divided among the natural sciences and everyone else. Overall, his chances were some miniscule fraction of 20%.

The effect of the new research expectations in Medway's case would be that he would be labelled a failure. He was still an active researcher, a productive publisher of articles, chapters and books, and an acknowledged expert in his field. But because he had no external grants, he would not meet the University's expectations.

He was somewhat consoled in this by the thought that hardly anyone else in the social sciences or humanities at Leichardt would meet the expectations. This even included several of the select band of Leichardt Distinguished Professors, who had been singled out as the University's leaders in research. They would all be failures together.

An even greater consolation was that some eminent figures in political theory would have been in similar difficulties. Plato and Aristotle secured few grants, although, it was true, they both sold their services, for a while, to political strongmen. The record of the Stoics and Cynics was completely unacceptable, their negative attitude to external funding worse even than Medway's. True, Hobbes, Locke and Rousseau had managed to get funding from private patrons, but only for themselves, not for any university. Machiavelli had a small patrimony and, for a while, was employed by the state. Hegel lived off his university income, Mill relied on his salary from the East India Company. Marx survived precariously on his earnings from journalism, which he supplemented by cadging off Engels – again, he wasn't a winner of competitive grants. Isaiah Berlin was an Oxford scholar at a time when Oxford scholars didn't even have to publish if they didn't feel like it, let alone pursue grant funding. Rawls came from a wealthy background, but did he win any grants? Medway would have to look that one up. All in all, the performance of the political theory greats was poor when it came to grants. They would not meet the expectations of Leichardt.

The consequences for those who did not meet the new expectations were unclear. Vaguely threatening things were said about the effect this would have on promotion, to which darker mutterings were added about the possibility of 'performance management further down the line.' Performance management was a process in which a person's work would be checked and assessed more frequently than usual, with the possibility of dismissal for persistent nonperformance. Perhaps especially intransigent cases would be thrown into the sea, weighed down by their own computers. None of this was spelled out.

The expectations were really an exercise in public shaming. Perhaps the next step would be that those who failed to meet the targets would have to wear a dunce's cap. A set of stocks might be set up in the CHQ. But shaming is more effective when individuals or minorities are singled out, rather than when everyone is told they should be ashamed of themselves, so it just might be that the performance expectations would have no real consequences. So many people would be labelled substandard that any penalties would have to be applied to virtually everyone – at least in the non-sciences – and that might prove awkward to accomplish, even for Murdo and Ethel. On the other hand, you wouldn't want to underestimate them, especially when it came to the punitive arts.

9

TEAM TALK

Murdo's inaugural speech and subsequent consultations had been no more than preliminaries. The official launch of his program took place in a gloomy reception room at the foot of the Citadel. All the executive deans, school deans and other worthies were invited, so Medway was in attendance along with Ethel, Professor Cardigan, Owen, and others. The centrepiece of the event was the issuing of a glossy Target 1 % brochure which distilled the essence of the reforms.

Medway collected his copy and took post between Owen and Alex Euripides, the Law dean. 'Looking forward to today's announcement from the Monarch of the Glum?' said Euripides.

'Can't wait. Fine-looking brochure, anyway.'

Opening the overproduced item, Medway read, with some surprise, that the University's new agenda was to be guided by 'a set of values.' He was about to read what these were when Murdo came to the lectern.

'When I represented Australia at cricket, and especially when I was captain,' he began, his prominent eyes misting over at the memory of those halcyon days, 'our team was always guided by a list of fundamental values. They gave us the moral compass we were known for internationally. Well, it's the same for universities. A university's values are its foundation.'

As a professional philosopher, Medway took a keen interest in what Leichardt's values would turn out to be. Would they reflect a sophisticated Millian form of utilitarianism, or Kantianism, or a statement of Aristotelian virtue ethics, or even an expression of Nietzschean will to power? It turned out that, in Murdo's view, 'five values in particular will be the foundation of our success.'

'Let me take you through them,' said Murdo, pointing to the text in the brochure where the values were listed as follows.

1. Student centred. This included imperatives to 'focus on student success' and 'empower students as partners.' Medway was surprised that focusing on student success should be regarded as a goal needing to be spelled out, since he could have sworn that he had been doing this for years. Empowering students as partners, on the other hand, overlooked what seemed an obvious truth, that the relation between a student and a teacher is not one of 'partnership' exactly, since in the relevant respects they are not equals. If, in the academic context, students were the equals of their teachers, they would not be students and their teachers would not be teachers.

2. Integrity. Here, Medway and his colleagues were urged to 'maintain the highest professional and ethical standards at all times', to 'be accountable for our actions and follow through on our commitments', and to 'treat others with courtesy and respect.' This sounded good, but it would be interesting to see how far Murdo and his supporters applied these standards to themselves.

3. Courage. Under this heading, the staff were told to 'trust and empower' (what or whom, exactly?), to 'seize opportunities and embrace change' (that seemed more likely, given the coming restructures), to 'learn from experience' (people did know what was coming, given Murdo's track record), to 'be open and transparent in our communications' (see 2, above), and to 'pursue critical and open inquiry' (Medway looked forward to inquiring critically and openly into Murdo's plans).

4. Innovation. This was a favourite theme of Murdo's. He loved the Centre for Innovation, which was run by a director with the thrusting, upbeat and empty personality of a snake-oil salesman – not unlike the current PM. On Murdo's watch, every student in the University had to take a mandatory Innovation course whether they wished to innovate or not. On this score, the staff were adjured to 'solve problems by "thinking outside the box"' – although, unfortunately, the overpaid media consultant who came up with that expression had not really thought outside the box. Another goal was to 'actively engage with business and industry', which really meant that the task of the University was to produce 'job-ready' graduates who could slot into the employment market with no further training – in other words, to do the work of business and industry for them.

5. Excellence. 'Strive for excellence in every endeavor,' the staff were told – presumably instead of working steadfastly towards mediocrity as they always had in the past.

'Are there any comments at this point?' asked Murdo.

Medway put his hand up. 'What about the value of the staff? That doesn't seem to be mentioned anywhere.'

'Oh, of course, the staff are the University's greatest asset,' said Murdo, obviously reciting a formula he'd learned by rote. 'And the value of the staff is acknowledged in *Target 1%*. In fact, it's so important that we've given it a section of its own, the "People and Culture" section on page 10. Let me read it to you.

> People are the heart of our university and it is the sum of their achievements that will deliver our vision and future success. Our culture must support and encourage those achievements and must value the positive contributions made by staff, students, alumni and council. Above all, we must always seek to inspire and enable the achievements of others.

Well, thought Medway, if the signs are correct, the achievements and contributions of the staff will soon be valued in new and unexpected ways, including the sudden ending of their careers. Presumably, that's an instance of 'thinking outside the box.'

'To underline this vision for our staff,' said Murdo, 'the Human Resources unit will be renamed "People and Culture."' This made little difference to Medway. Prior to the Bodkin affair he'd had the naïve idea that Human Resources was some kind of impartial defender of the University's rules and processes. Post-Bodkin, he realised that their role was simply to back up whatever had been decided, however wrongly, by senior management. Ever since then he'd thought of Human Resources as 'Human Instruments,' and that was unlikely to change.

'Furthermore,' Murdo continued, 'there will be a Deputy Vice-Chancellor (People and Culture) and a Vice-President of People of Culture.'

'What's the difference?' inquired Professor Euripides, somewhat abruptly.

'The DVC will be an academic appointment, and the Vice-President will be from the administrative staff.'

'But why do we need them both?' Euripides pursued. 'They sound like Tweedledum and Tweedledee.'

'Sorry, what's your name?' Murdo asked.

'Alex Euripides, from Law.'

Murdo appeared to be consulting a notebook, using a pen to guide his convex eye over a list and eventually stopping when he seemed to find what he was looking for.

'Ah, yes, Professor Euripides,' said Murdo. 'The DVCPC and the VPPC have quite different jobs.'

'Yes, but what are they?'

Murdo fixed Euripides with the kind of glare, combining contempt with menace, that he used to reserve for England batsmen.

'The DVCPC formulates People and Culture policy, in consultation with the senior executive and the Council, and the VPPC *executes* the policy.' The emphasis Murdo gave to that last verb left the audience in no doubt as to what he would like done with Euripides.

'And now, if there are no further questions about the values …'

But the Director of the Red Centre for Indigenous Studies had his hand up.

'Yes, Professor Motlop?'

'They're all very white,' said Motlop.

'Sorry, what are very white?'

'The values. They're all very white.'

Murmured conversations suddenly stopped, replaced by a shocked silence. This was awkward. Murdo wriggled visibly with discomfort, his eyes protruding somewhat. Medway could see his difficulty. Murdo could ask which of the values were especially white, and why, and perhaps go on to suggest that they might all be values suitable for any university. But then he would appear to be unsympathetic with the concerns of the Red Centre.

'Ah, yes, well, yes,' he stammered. 'It may be … It's possible, I suppose, … that our existing values are not, er, wholly comprehensive. Good point, yes. I can assure you that the University will maintain a watching brief on the matter.'

In the audience, murmuring recommenced. Euripides winked at Medway and whispered that the whiteness of the values, whatever that meant, was the least of their problems.

But Murdo wasn't finished. 'Good, thank you,' he said, evidently relieved that the worst had passed. That sudden attack by Motlop had been unnerving. It reminded Murdo of batting on the ridge at Lords – or at any rate witnessing the destruction from the non-striker's end – when Dobbs was taking 8/29. But the danger had passed and now he was going to take the long handle to these bastards. 'We'll move on to another initiative,' he said.

At his signal, flunkeys brought in a series of cardboard boxes. For a moment, Medway wondered whether Murdo had somehow caused the five values of the University to take material form so that they could be more easily comprehended and measured by the natural scientists.

'Another thing I learned from my experience of elite sport,' said Murdo, 'is the vital importance of teamwork. We didn't win the Ashes three times running under my captaincy without all being on the same page, all dedicated to the same goals. It's the same in business. Everyone in the company must unite in pursuing the goals of the company.'

'So,' he signalled to the flunkeys, who began opening the boxes, 'a corporate ethos is important. Everyone has to feel part of the team. In academia there's been too much emphasis on outmoded notions such as "academic freedom", which really just means the freedom of individuals to get in the way of team effort. This has certainly been true at Leichardt. As a first step towards a more team-oriented approach, we're bringing in more of a corporate look.'

Reaching into one of the boxes, Murdo extracted and held up a red, one-size-fits-all baseball cap with an adjustable plastic strap at the back. On the front of the cap, a message was picked out in white letters. It read, 'Make Leichardt Great.' Delving into another box, Murdo extracted a white T-shirt bearing the same logo in red.

'Make Leichardt Great!' boomed Murdo in triumph. 'I think you'll agree that we'll all be proud to wear this cap or this T-shirt as we go about our daily work for the University. From now on, I want to see all staff members wearing the Make Leichardt Great cap or T-shirt during lectures, tutorials, meetings, and in general on any ordinary university business.'

A wave of alarm and muttering passed across the room as the academics came to terms with what had been said. Eventually a hand was raised. It was Professor Toynbee, the historian.

'Have you lost your mind?' Toynbee inquired. 'This is a university, not the changing rooms of some bunch of juveniles in a state of permanently arrested development.'

'I'm sorry you feel that way,' Murdo replied evenly, checking his notebook again. 'I'm only trying to instill a sense of team identity. That's how we'll get to the top 1%. It's a pity you can't see that, and it's a shame you have to disrespect the national sport.'

'Yes, Professor Toynbee,' Ethel piped up from the front row, 'Shame on you. The Vice-Chancellor is only thinking of the good of the University.'

'Thank you, Ethel,' said Murdo, forcing his grim features to project in her direction something approximating to a smile. 'But I appreciate there may be some people whose, what should I call it, "personal style" may be offended by a humble baseball cap – even if it is, as I like to think, the baggy green of Leichardt. And I also realise that there may be more formal occasions – conferences, meetings with representatives of industry and other stakeholders, scouting for enrolments and research talent overseas, and so on – where our corporate look needs to be more formal.'

Murdo paused as he reached into another box, this time removing a navy-blue jacket. It had yellow piping along its edges and, on its breast-pocket, the Leichardt crest. Medway had never studied the crest carefully before, but when the jacket was passed around he could see an emu and a kangaroo holding up a shield featuring a pioneer or explorer – probably meant to be the ill-fated Leichhardt – trying to read a document (possibly a map?) by the dim light of the Southern Cross. On the scroll there was the motto, 'Leichardt illuminatio mea.' Medway thought he could design something more contemporary. The shield's supporters should be a scientist in a lab coat on one side and a banker in a pin-stripe suit on the other. The shield itself would depict a desert waste, empty except for a set of footprints leading to a giant dollar sign on the horizon. The scroll should read, in the phrase Owen was so fond of, 'Show me the money.'

'So, for more formal people and occasions,' Murdo continued, 'we've designed a Leichardt corporate blazer. This is a prototype, just to show you what it looks like. Smart, isn't it? We'll be getting in touch with all staff individually to take orders and measurements. Again, this is not optional; it's University policy. We'll expect every staff member to have the full set of cap, T-shirt and blazer. At least one of these must be worn at all times on University business. We'll be asking you to pay for the cost of the T-shirt and blazer – they will be tax-deductible, of course. The Make Leichardt Great cap will be free!'

Discussion resumed, opinion divided between those, like Ethel, who supported the Vice-Chancellor's inspiring initiative, and those, like Toynbee, who thought he was clinically insane. Professor Tennyson, from English, obscurely muttered something about 'sartor resartus.' As Murdo afterwards expressed it to his executive assistant, Courtney, 'Christ knows what the old prick was talking about.' But, as usual, it didn't matter what anyone said because the corporate look had been decreed by Murdo and was therefore University policy.

In the coming weeks, everyone received their caps and everyone was asked to send in their T-shirt and blazer measurements. Some complied, others did not. Whelper, for example, was delighted to be seen to be on board with the policy, at every opportunity wearing not just one but all three official garments simultaneously, making him look like the lead guitarist from AC/DC. On the other hand, Medway joined the dissenters, refusing to wear any of the items under any circumstances, and even declining to send in his measurements.

Murdo's 'corporate look' edict thus had the effect of dividing the staff into two visible classes, the pro- and anti-Murdo. There were also other more indeterminate categories. Moderates wore one of the items but not the others. Waverers sent in their measurements but then couldn't bring themselves to put the things on, or sometimes wore the items and sometimes didn't. There were even radicals, who met at CHQ where they made a show of cutting up and burning the articles in public.

As in the case of the research expectations, the consequences of non-compliance with the corporate look were unclear. For the present, the non-compliant suffered no penalty. But there was a sense that there would be a reckoning eventually. For one thing, it was now easy to spot who had chosen which side.

10

ATTRITION

'We see that the rate of attrition for *Introduction to Modern Ideologies* is in excess of the expected maximum. Do you have any response, Geoff?'

The Chair of the Faculty's Knowledge Delivery Committee was a reasonable person and he was just doing his job. His Leichardt blazer identified him as a collaborator, but that shouldn't be held against him personally – everyone had to deal with Murdo's regime as they thought fit. Still, Medway had little patience with the attrition issue.

'Not really,' he said. 'Everyone knows there are various reasons for attrition. A lot of our students are not really prepared for university work and don't know what they're doing here. Others are not really here at all; they've only enrolled so they can keep their welfare payments coming. Some start off okay but change their minds and want to do something else. My view is that the students are adults, and whether they choose to stay or go or never turn up is their business.'

'Geoff, I sympathise with what you're saying but, as you know, student attrition is a matter of concern for the University. Reducing attrition is University policy.'

This was true. Not, of course, because of any great pedagogical principle but because each student who withdrew represented money walking out the door. Consequently, working groups had been set up to monitor rates of attrition and try to lower them. At one point it was proposed that lecturers with attriting students – yes, 'to attrit' was now a verb – would ring them up in the evenings to find out why they were attriting and beg them to return. Nick said he was prepared to do this. This time-consuming and futile policy was actually put into effect, but fortunately for the academic staff the task was given to the admin staff – unfortunately for them.

'May I ask something?' said Medway.

'Of course.'

'Who says our attrition rate of 25% is "excessive"? The current maximum is 20%, right? How is that calculated?'

'That's the figure Ethel has decided on.'

'No doubt, but how? By what process of evidence and reasoning did she arrive at it?'

'Sorry, I can't say. Ethel just gave us the figure.'

'Let me put the question in another way. Ethel must have got the figure from somewhere. From which orifice, do you think?'

The committee secretary, typing away on her laptop, sniggered. Oh well, thought Medway, at least that question would enliven the minutes. Still, he realised he was taking a risk saying things like this in public. He had even heard rumours that Murdo was making a 'hit list' of troublemakers. Surely, that couldn't be true. Could it?

***

Returning to the deanery, Medway positioned the box of tissues within easy reach, ready for the next meeting. This time it would be Karen, the School office manager.

Murdo's agenda called for the restructuring of the admin staff first. One by one, they were scheduled to be detached from their current jobs in the doomed schools and either 'redeployed' elsewhere in the University – in another phrase they were to be 'mapped over' – or handed redundancy notices. Their actual mapping or removal was to take place later; for the time being they would stay at their present posts. But their fate was sealed.

Karen had assembled the School office team, replacing the coven of witches who had run the office previously. The first school manager had come from the north of England, combining the voice of Johnny Vegas and with the manner of an officer in the SS. She had filled the school office with a kind of netball mafia, everyone being connected to the game somehow. This in itself wasn't objectionable to Medway (Sarah had played netball), but most of the mafia seemed also to have been selected for their possession of the most disagreeable personality possible. The slightest request for help tended to be greeted with disdainful dismissal or pouting resentment. The general view of the netball mafia was that the

University's function was the fulfilment of routine administrative tasks, from which teaching and research were irritating distractions. Fortunately, the original manager had been promoted to something in central administration, where her personality was more likely to be regarded as a virtue. She was succeeded by Karen, who proved to be a warm, nurturing person, like a mother hen. Karen got rid of the netball mafia and replaced it with a new team of people who actually wanted to be helpful.

Now the School's excellent team of administrators was taken apart piece by piece. Astrid, Medway's PA, was to be transferred to general duties down in the Faculty (soon to be College) Labyrinth. Deirdre, the finance officer, would be sent away to work in a subterranean cavern somewhere in central administration. Jill, who assisted where necessary, saw what was coming, resigned and took a job in one of the universities in the CBD.

Karen's was the most painful case. Although subjected to numerous interviews, she could not be redeployed. Once the schools were abolished, there would be no need for school managers. Her only option was redundancy.

This bleak prospect was to be laid on the line for her at an interview conducted by Gertrude Strappado, the cypher from Human Instruments who had helped Ethel to dispatch Ki-Lee Bodkin. As Karen's supervisor, Medway was there with her, and the interview was held in his office. Marshalling all her native tact and charm, Gertrude mechanically read out the relevant procedures from the 'change management' handbook. Karen was reduced to tears; Medway passed her the tissues.

***

The next morning, Medway entered his office, turned his computer on and opened his email inbox. With the usual feeling of dread, he scrolled down to the latest message from Ethel. Her practice was to fire off most of her emails at around 6 pm. This left recipients with an awkward choice. They could take a peek straight away and risk ruining their evening, or they could avoid looking until the following morning and have less time to respond to whatever imperative was being issued. This time Medway had opted to wait until morning.

A chill wind was blowing in his direction from the Bunker. Messages were terser, more peremptory, and carried a nasty undertone. Of course, Medway had long been expecting this; now his expectation was starting to be borne out. What was the cause? It was hard to be sure, since all of Medway's recent communication with Ethel was by the impersonal medium of email. The weekly one-to-one meetings had petered out. That may have been because Ethel was too busy constructing the new College in her own image. The doomed School of Social Studies, along with its dean, was an irrelevance. But Medway also had the sense that he had finally used up whatever personal capital he might once have had with Ethel. The social work battles – in particular, over the Masters numbers and Bodkin's case – had probably taken their toll. Perhaps that comment about the orificial origins of Ethel's attrition policy had got back to her?

Anyway, it was with a weary sense of imminent pain that Medway clicked on Ethel's name in his inbox. The day before, she had sent him a brusque demand for some documents to do with staff workload, couched in gnomic terms that left him unsure of what exactly she wanted. He had asked for clarification. Now he had Ethel's response.

'If you can't understand what I'm asking,' the message read, 'you shouldn't be a school dean.' Well, he probably shouldn't be a school dean, for various reasons. At any rate, he was clearly well on the way to being consigned to the outer darkness. His main consolation was that he would be joining a lot of distinguished company.

***

Owen, for instance. In the afternoon Owen called and asked Medway to meet him at the usual coffee and smoking place behind Hayek South. There he wasted no time getting to the point.

'Geoff, I resigned this morning,' he said, sucking the cigarette fumes savagely into his lungs. 'I'll be gone by the end of the day.'

'Christ, what's happened?'

Things had been happening for some time. There had been the Jose Escondido affair, the calls in the middle of the night, the vicious attacks when things went wrong because of decisions Ethel had made herself, the habitual rudeness and lack of empathy.

The last straw was the case of Professor Toynbee. Medway had last seen Toynbee at the Vice-Chancellor's team-talk when Murdo had revealed the new corporate look. Toynbee had not been kind about it. Not long after this he decided to retire, requesting adjunct status so he could continue to use the Library and other resources for his research. Historically, the granting of adjunct status was a matter of course. In Toynbee's case, the Faculty stood only to gain from granting him the status, since he regularly produced a book every five years or so, which was more than respectable. If he was placed on the adjunct list, his publications would continue to be credited to the Faculty and University, which would qualify for public research funding accordingly.

Toynbee's application came to Owen because History was, for some reason it would take a historian to unravel, part of Owen's School of International Studies. Owen approved the application without a second thought. Ethel also approved, although not in writing, and Owen told Toynbee that everything was fine.

But then Owen, on a student recruitment junket in China with Ethel, received a text from Toynbee. He had been told by Human Instruments to hand in his entry-card and key, and be off the campus by close of business on Friday. Otherwise, he would be stripped naked, frog-marched to the exit, and possibly tasered by an overweight security guard. He emailed Ethel, asking her to confirm his academic status so he could hold onto his card, key, and underpants. There was no reply. Oh Christ, Owen thought, here we go again.

'Ethel, have you heard from Professor Toynbee regarding confirmation of his academic status? I told him it had been verbally confirmed to me, so perhaps …'

'I changed my mind!' Owen recalled Ethel's triumphant, defiant expression, like a six-year-old who has grabbed all the marbles and won't give them back.

'I see. How come?'

'He's never liked me since I arrived, and he's tried to undermine me from day one. He's not a team player: his opposition to Target 1% is intolerable. He can ride off into the sunset.'

Toynbee did ride off, writing his books and attracting research funding for one of Leichardt's competitors downtown.

Owen rode off too.

'Who needs this?' he said. 'This time I'm out of academia altogether. I'm going to become a tradie.'

A tradie? Owen was given to overstatement for dramatic effect, and surely this was an example. There had been a character in the old Politics department, Don Winter, who had pretended to be a tradie, wearing a blue singlet and tan moleskins, driving about in a Hilux ute, and speaking in a faux-Ocker dialect. This was all intended to show political solidarity with the working class. Owen, by contrast, had little time for the working class, once remarking that 'we should get them before they get us', so the tradie idea seemed unlikely. How could a professor of international political theory end up driving a ute, failing to keep appointments, sending in opaque quotes, and grossly overcharging for his services?

But this time, true to his word, Owen moved with his family back to Queensland and went into business painting houses. Ethel had that effect on people.

***

It was the School's farewell lunch, and the bar in the Client Services Building was packed. Penny-pinching to the end, the Faculty would not contribute anything towards the event, but there was enough in the School kitty to make it worthwhile. People bought their own drinks, some quite a few.

Medway looked out over the familiar faces. Millicent, conversing at stentorian levels, was haranguing Professor Cardigan about some aspect of patriarcho-capitalist perfidy. Pleonexia was letting Nola the Flamingo into some secret and Nick was patiently listening to Whelper's stories about the famous politicians he was intimate with. Even Plume was present, although looking pale. Alas, this was the last time they'd all be together like this.

Medway tapped on a glass to get their attention. 'A few final words before we all go our separate ways,' he said. Out of his jacket pocket he fished his speaking notes, recorded on index-cards. He thanked everyone for their work, singling out a few especially deserving souls, and expressed their shared disappointment. But he wanted to end on a lighter note and recited a poem he'd written especially for the occasion. It was of doubtful quality, but it was the best he could do.

God did not create Leichardt,
He got it from Professor Pound.
Alas it was sans form and void,
Of sense there was no sight or sound.
Well, that is not entirely true,
It did not lack for form,
Too many forms were our disgrace,
Red tape was on the uni's face.

And then: "A survey let there be!"
God saw the survey – it was good,
It echoed all that He believed.
"Restructure now there must proceed."
Some doubted that there was a need,
They claimed there was no fitting wound.
Their wrongness was just plain to see
Because the survey so decreed.

In the Garden of Eden abode a school,
Studying some social matters.
They claimed they needed no reform
Boasting some high-scoring batters.
And God addressed them with these words:
"Ye should not be so pleased withal.
Ye meet some targets but not all,
Forsooth, ye quite flat-line in grants –
In that respect ye do appall.
Who differently thinks is good and fine
Unless his hopes do not align.

Losers like that shall straight be tossed,
And from all redeployment lost."

And God proceeded with His plan.
He started with his power-base:
A firmament was set in place.
Its stars enhanced the uni's lustre –
It was the key to the restructure.
We're talking the senior executive here,
A mafia ruled by greed and fear.

God then reordered the admin staff –
Or "mapped them over" for a laugh.
Their desks would face in the same direction,
That would prevent any dereliction.

All this took some four long days.
Day five God named his salary,
Uncountable by you and me,
But on it he was fully bent
To reach the topmost 1%.

He tackled the academics next
And faculties became colleges
He settled on the number – six.
The lot would be ruled by a bunch of pricks.
Their duty to complete the task.
On such details God wasn't arsed.

He rested on the seventh day
Further duties ducked,
Leaving some to then observe
"Leichardt's completely fucked!"

But what of the School of Social Studies?
Alas, it was expelled
From the Garden where it had dwelt,
Its talents quite dispelled.
And then some natural tears were shed
But they hoped for the best,
The world was all before them laid,
To choose their place of rest,
Or be mapped over to new posts,
Or else converted into ghosts.

Thus fated now, they hand in hand,
With wandering steps and slow,
Through Eden made their different ways,
And some had far to go.
The diaspora spread far and wide,
For God did not relent,
But Providence became their guide,
Or Target 1%.

11

PANOPTICON

The old order passed away. The School of Social Studies was 'disestablished', along with every other school. Medway received a form letter from Ethel thanking him for his service as 'dean of the School of International Studies.' No doubt he was interchangeable with the other pawns.

The new order was born. Ethel became the Vice President and Executive Dean of the new College of Non-Sciences, which consisted of the Humanities, Social Sciences (including Government and Women's Studies but minus Psychology and Social Work, which went to the new College of Social Control), Business, and Law. Few were delighted by the new arrangement. No one wanted to be in bed with Business, an unattractive, unproductive and flatulent companion. Law was understandably upset at the loss of its status as a distinct school. Its last dean, Alex Euripides, had pleaded for its retention, if only as a label, arguing that it was necessary for accreditation purposes. Ethel rejected that idea out of hand, smelling in it the foul stench of decentralisation and self-determination. Naturally, at the mention of accreditation, she was backed up by the University's central administration.

The Government component of the new college was led by Nigel Plume and his deputy Pleonexia Self. Somewhat against the general current of bold innovation, the Government set-up included two features that revived the past in peculiar ways. First, Politics was reunited with its long-lost brother, International Relations. Years before, they had been uneasy bedfellows in the old Politics department, before personal animosities had led to their separation by Roy Beadle into different schools. Now that many of the original bellige-rents on both sides had moved on, having either retired or expired, they were back together again. Apparently, the School of International Studies, touted by Beadle as poten-tially a 'vibrant' centre of teaching and research, had not been so vibrant after all. It was permanently in the red, in spite of Owen's best efforts.

Second, Beadle stepped down from his eminence as Deputy Vice-Chancellor (Academic) and returned to the new Government unit as an ordinary professor. Contrary to most expectations, he had not reached the summit after all, having applied for the position of Vice-Chancellor twice and been rejected both times. In Murdo's regime he had continued for a while but eventually decided to resign, replaced by the up-and-coming Prudence Climber, the former Deputy Vice-Chancellor (Students).

Medway spotted him in the corridor one afternoon and couldn't resist. 'Hi Roy. Back from Syracuse?'

Beadle looked understandably puzzled. 'Hello, Geoff. No, I've never been there.'

'Sorry, Roy, it's a philosopher's in-joke. Plato tried for a while to advise Dionysius, the Tyrant of Syracuse, before he eventually gave it up as a bad job.'

'Ah, I see what you mean. Very good,' said Beadle, awkwardly forcing his sad features to try on a smile as if it were a jumper he knew would be too small. Medway decided not to mention that the Syracuse phrase had also been used by someone greeting Heidegger after he'd returned from serving the Nazi party as Rector of Freiburg University.

Instead, he said, 'You must have had a difficult time recently.'

'No more difficult than usual.' Beadle was giving little away, but the rumours (notably propagated by Pleonexia) were that his aspirations had turned out to be imperfectly aligned with Target 1%. It was an open question on what precise point he had parted company with Murdo's crusade, especially since he had himself instituted many changes that had prepared the way for it. Did he now regret these? Beadle was not saying.

Resigning from Murdo's administration was one thing; it was an even greater mystery why Beadle had come back to Hayek South. After finishing as a senior executive, the usual course would be for him to fold his tent and steal off into the night. He would be dignified by the title, 'Emeritus Professor', signifying his sterling service over many years. Yet here he was. Ethel gave him an enormous office befitting his distinguished standing. In other respects he received no special treatment. Indeed, Ethel took enormous pleasure in piling work onto him with little allowance for his transitional disadvantages. Even though he had not been in a classroom for a decade, he was immediately given a full teaching load, complete with courses he had never taught before and mountains of undergraduate marking. This he absorbed without complaint, saying only that he was thrilled to be back teaching again, as if daring Ethel to do her worst.

On the other hand, Beadle was perversely prevented from doing certain kinds of work he wanted to do. Learning that such a senior professor was suddenly in their midst, numerous graduate students applied to be supervised by him. But the University had now instituted a set of strict new rules about who could supervise. In order to qualify, the supervisor had to have achieved, within the previous five years, minimum numbers of research publications and graduate completions. Beadle did not meet these requirements because for the last decade he had spent every waking minute chairing meetings, writing memos, tightening majors and closing loopholes.

Besieged by students wanting his help, Beadle asked Ethel if she would agree to relax the rules while he got his research moving again. His argument seemed reasonable that he had simply not had the opportunity, within the relevant timeframe, to satisfy the supervision qualifications. He would do so if he was given a year or two to catch up. Weeks later, a reply eventually arrived from the College's new dean of Human Instruments, Dicky Sediment, a lazy and self-important functionary Ethel had imported from the UK. The answer was no. The upshot was that one of the most experienced and distinguished political scientists in Australia was deemed unqualified to supervise graduate students.

Experiences like these had humanised Beadle, it seemed to Medway. He seemed more relaxed and more inclined to see things from the perspective of the rank-and-file staff. After all, that was his own situation now. For the first time in twenty-five years he was not in a leadership position but a lecturer and tutor like everyone else.

Not quite like everyone else: he possessed an unrivalled knowledge of the University's rules and procedures. The result was that he became a kind of all-purpose behind-the-scenes adviser, dispenser of wisdom and comforter for those who found themselves crushed in the jaws of either Ethel or the University – that is, just about everyone at one time or another. Beadle had changed from being a remote and pitiless ruler into a genuinely human resource of great value. Murdo and Ethel had, unwittingly, created a monster.

***

With the end of his time as dean, Medway was expelled from the managerial grandeur of the deanery (incidentally losing his reserved space in Carpark 13) and given another office in Hayek South. It was smaller but still of generous, professorial dimensions, so he couldn't complain in that respect. It was also on the north side of the building, which was no bad thing in itself. North-facing aspects were highly prized in the city's real estate. The best of the light came from the north, especially during winter. The trouble was that, although Medway's new room was on the building's north side, it was not north facing. For the first time, he found himself facing inward to the quad at the building's centre. The room did not get a lot of light; its gloominess, compared with Medway's previous accommodations, was noticeable straight away.

Moreover, there was the matter of the view. His earlier, outward-facing rooms had afforded a succession of agreeable prospects. When he had arrived at Leichardt, he started on the east side overlooking the sea. On making professor, he progressed to Beadle's old office on the south side, with its view of gum trees. After that came the deanery on the west side, and the panoptic vista of Carpark 13. Even when he had been in the temporary quarters while the refurbishment was proceeding, he had enjoyed a pleasant view from higher up in the tree of knowledge than before or since.

By contrast, the new view inward to the Hayek South quad was deeply depressing. Before the refurbishment, the quad had been packed with luxuriant, even chaotic foliage, some of it as tall as the three stories of the building. It was like a Brazilian rain forest – the Yanomami would have felt at home there. Some people thought they saw monkeys swinging from the trees, although that was probably just the undergraduates. There had been a pond in the centre, admittedly somewhat stagnant, but providing a welcome water feature.

The remodelling swept all this away. The old jungle was replaced by mounds of dirt where lawns had been sown but not yet developed, and a few immature shrubs corralled within small, square beds with concrete edges. Instead of the pond, there was now a similarly cement-bound basin in which a tiny pool of water percolated feebly. To look down onto the quad was to see something akin to a desert. It was the kind of barren wilderness that had killed Leichhardt the explorer.

Nor was there much relief to be gained from looking across to the other side of the building. There Medway was confronted by a wall of concrete brutalism relieved only by the narrow, black slits of office windows, the kind of aperture through which defenders might have poured boiling oil in the Middle Ages. Somewhere down on the ground floor, at the back of the teaching rooms and secure behind the College's card-entry system, was Ethel's Bunker.

There was something prison-like about Medway's new outlook. The three stories of concrete suggested the high walls of a penitentiary, the empty quad an exercise yard. Medway imagined a siren sounding and a file of academics shuffling around in leg-irons, marking student essays and applying for grants as they went. For the first time he could see the airconditioning structures on the roof. Armed guards might be patrolling up there.

As in the deanery, Medway was put in mind of Bentham's panopticon, the model prison in which prisoners could be kept under constant surveillance by guards who themselves could not be seen. Only, this time he felt more like an inmate than a guard. There was, of course, no guard tower in the centre of the quad as there had been in Bentham's design. Still, Medway had the feeling that from some featureless window opposite, Ethel and her underlings might well be watching.

The whole experience gave Medway a new and unexpected sympathy with Foucault – or 'Foucoo', as his former PhD student, Harriet Credopol (who had found another supervisor) had insisted on pronouncing it. Since his last encounter with that great genius (Foucault, not Harriet), he had not changed his mind about some matters. He still believed that Foucault's reduction of morality to power was, by definition, ethically bankrupt. But his new window on the Hayek South panopticon gave him a fresh interest in Foucault's account of power.

What was interesting was not anything in Foucault's shallow and self-defeating analysis, it was his imagery. From Medway's new perspective, the French lunatic did seem to capture something viscerally true in his metaphorical use of the panopticon. Unlike Bentham, who saw things through the eyes of the authorities, Foucault emphasised the point of view of the incarcerated. These are people who live under conditions in which they may be under surveillance at any moment without knowing exactly when. They end up policing themselves, internalising the norms of the prison, which become part of who they are. The general picture is of a dimension of power that consists not in outright and visible force or coercion but in the invisible inculcation of norms through surveillance, or the permanent possibility of surveillance, alone.

According to Foucault, this is true not just of Bentham's model prison but of modern society as a whole. We all live in a panopticon or 'carceral' society whose norms are invisibly insinuated in us by a range of institutions managed by experts in 'the human sciences' – doctors, psychiatrists, psychologists, social workers, political scientists, and so on – who have themselves been conditioned by the institutions.

The question for Medway, as he stared out over the desiccated quad in the direction of the Bunker, was whether Leichardt had turned into just another branch of Foucault's panopticon society. There seemed good reason to answer yes. There was certainly plenty of surveillance and internalising of norms going on. Murdo's Target 1% was in essence a system of this kind, with its concern for world rankings and the measuring of performance against key indicators. Woe betide those who did not measure up (sic) to these norms. They would be seen to have 'aspirations that no longer align with those of the University', in the lapidary phrase Murdo had made his own. To avoid this fate, people had to embrace the University's program to the point of making it part of their personal identity. Those who did not include among their life goals the securing of external research grants were not proper people.

Foucault's metaphor also seemed to capture another dimension of Medway's predicament: its impersonal character made it intractable. One of Foucault's most famous pronouncements, often urged on Medway by Nick, is that 'We need to cut off the King's head: in political theory that has still to be done.' The idea is that there is a sense in which power is not the possession or instrument of anyone in particular, but rather an impersonal network or process within which people are situated like nodes, both acted upon and constructed (through the internalisation of norms) by the circuitry within which they find themselves.

This side of Foucault answered to the sense Medway had of being caught in a web of power, the details of which he was only dimly aware, and from which there was no escape. To escape from a system of power, you need to oppose it, and to oppose it you need to track it to its source. But what was the source of power in the Leichardt panopticon? Ethel seemed to have power, but she was the instrument of Murdo, so maybe the real power rested with him. But Murdo could be seen as merely reacting to the federal government's refusal to provide adequate funding for higher education. Even the government was pushed along by the external forces of globalised neoliberal political economy. It was hard to locate any particular person or institution with sufficient responsibility for what was going on to make it a suitable target even for complaint let alone active opposition.

Yet, there is something deeply unsatisfactory and frustrating about this kind of thinking. It is unsatisfactory because Ethel and Murdo really did possess power, and they really did use it as an instrument of their own idiosyncratic wishes. It is frustrating because, if you accept the whole Foucauldian package, what are you supposed to do? There is no room left for agency. Even your own will and wishes turn out to be driven by norms internalised from the power circuit within which you're trapped. So, where do you go from there? The Foucauldian images of the panopticon and the impersonal web of power are striking and (as Steven Lukes says) 'seductive', but what next?

Foucault suggests that every instance of power brings with it something like automatic resistance. The norms you accept imply an alternative set of norms which you might otherwise accept. There is some truth in this, if one may use the dreaded word 'truth' in connection with Foucault. Down in the quad, the prevailing environment of faceless modernism was challenged by an interesting and charming development. The small water feature that had replaced the pond became home to a family of garden gnomes. Presumably, they were placed there by students; the staff was another possibility, but most of them were too afraid to do anything that smacked of rebellion. Then again, the gnomes always arrived under cover of darkness, so it could have been the staff. From time to time Ethel's lanyarded lackies would come and take the gnomes away, but as soon as that happened a new set of gnomes would appear. After a while, Ethel gave up and left the gnomes where they were.

What did the gnomes represent? It was hard to say. Possibly, they were effigies of Murdo, Climber, Ethel et al – certainly, their features distinctly resembled those of several members of the senior management. It did not really matter. Whatever they represented in the minds of their sponsors, they were clearly not authorised by Target 1%. There was a lightness, imaginativeness and irony about them that implied a sensibility that was utterly alien to the world of Murdo and Ethel.

On the other hand, the gnomes were hardly revolutionary. They were not going to change anything. At best, they were mute witnesses to an agenda that was more absurd, and far more harmful, than they were.

12

EFFICIENCY DIVIDEND

In his palatial office in the Citadel, Murdo leaned back in his chair, resting his feet on the desk with a sigh of contentment. From this position he could admire his new Salvatore Ferragamo alligator shoes. They'd set him back twenty grand, but what the hell, he could afford them. More to the point, he deserved them, since he was making such good progress with Target 1%.

Highlights included the following. He had abolished fourteen functioning schools, absorbing them into a series of colleges that would be governed by his own appointments. This would be a more streamlined arrangement, unimpeded by any bastions of local autonomy or by people who knew much about the fields they presided over. He had also rid Leichardt of a substantial number of its most competent admin staff, either deliberately, leaving them nowhere to be mapped over to, or inadvertently, making them so frightened or disgusted that they left for other jobs of their own accord.

The survivors huddled in confusion at their new locations in a system in which no one knew who was responsible for what.

But his favourite achievement was his inculcation of an ethos of unity and teamwork through the introduction of the corporate look. True, not everyone was on board with this. There were still staff members, academics in particular, non-scientists more especially, who were drifting around campus dressed in their usual slovenly outfits, as if they were free agents going about their own lives rather than members of a team. On the other hand, the policy had supporters, and he would find ways of getting the others to be team players rather than anarchists.

All of this was unquestionably $1.2 million worth of work, but Murdo was not finished yet. The restructuring of the academic staff lay ahead. Like the employees of the various companies he had taken over in the past, they would soon be applying for their own jobs. But before that happened, he wanted to consolidate his gains and implement some other ideas. That's what he wanted to talk through with his visitor this afternoon.

The phone rang; it was Courtney, his executive assistant. 'Professor Korova is here.'

'Thanks, Courtney, please send her in.' That Courtney had a very sexy voice, but he needed to focus. He'd asked Ethel to come and see him to talk over some policy options. She was a repulsive harpy but had also emerged as a useful ally, with the right attitude. He liked the way she had come to his aid in the debate with that arsehole from History. He had also heard good things about the way she was handling the ranks of losers who infested her College.

Ethel came in and Murdo waved her to a chair at his large meeting table, made of imported Norwegian pine. He joined her there.

'Thanks for coming, Ethel. How are you?'

'I'm well, thanks, Murdo. It's good to see you settling in so well and making such good progress with Target 1%.'

'Thanks, Ethel. We've done a great job but there's a lot more to be done. That's why I've asked you here. I'd like your advice on what our next moves should be.'

'Of course. Anything to help.'

'Okay. The first question is about the corporate look. We've declared the look to be University policy, and a lot of people are complying, especially the admin staff and the natural scientists. That's fine. But many people are not complying, especially among the Non-Sciences. I still see people teaching and coming to meetings without wearing any of the mandatory gear.'

'That's true, and it's disappointing. We have some very awkward people at Leichardt.'

'Right. My question is, do you have any ideas about how we can deal with that?'

Ethel had expected this question. 'Yes, Murdo, I do. I suggest you tie the corporate outfit to the recording of lectures: if the lecturer isn't wearing a blazer, or at least a T-shirt or cap, there'll be no online recording.'

'Okay, but where will that get us?'

'Well,' said Ethel – really, the man was a bit slow on the uptake – 'a course with no online recording will get fewer enrolments. That's because our students demand that their course be recorded online so they can access them when it's convenient. If it's not online, they won't sign up. And a course with fewer enrolments will be more likely to be caught by the University's "small course" rule.'

'The small course rule?'

Jesus, didn't he know anything? 'The small course rule says that if a course doesn't reach a minimum number of enrolments, it has to be cancelled for the semester. If that happens more than twice, the course is permanently discontinued.'

'I see,' said Murdo. Plainly, he didn't. 'But if the course is cancelled or discontinued, aren't we just excusing the lecturer from his – or her – teaching duties? Then they can just do as they like!' The idea of university lecturers doing as they liked made Murdo feel almost physically ill.

Ethel paused for a moment. The man knew nothing whatever about how a university works. Well, that's what you get when you appointed someone like Murdo. Still, you had to remember he had other virtues, or uses.

'No, Murdo, people whose courses are cancelled don't get to do what they like,' said Ethel, speaking slowly so the President and Vice-Chancellor could understand. 'In fact, quite the opposite. Everyone has to do a certain amount of work as measured by their unit's workload plan. So, if their course is cancelled they have to make up for it in other ways. And that's what we want. Instead of allowing them to teach these pissant course they're in love with, we can make them do other things – more profitable things – such as tutoring and marking in larger courses, or more administration.'

'Oh, I see what you're saying,' said Murdo, the penny finally dropping. 'We can use the small course rule to reinforce the corporate look. If they want to keep teaching their usual crap, they have to wear the official clobber. Otherwise, their enrolments will fall below the small course line because they're not going to be recorded online. So, this will force more people to wear the clobber.'

'That's it!'

'But also,' Murdo felt he was getting the hang of this, 'the corporate look reinforces the small course rule. Because if they don't wear the clobber, then we'll have a better chance of nailing them with the rule.'

'Exactly.' Perhaps he wasn't so dumb after all.

'Thanks, Ethel, that's fantastic. I'll get the troops to formulate the policy and make an announcement.'

'You're welcome, Murdo, glad to be of help.'

'You have been. And perhaps you can help me with another idea I've had.'

'Of course.' God, what could this be? Murdo's having an idea was a worrying prospect.

'Well, it's always struck me how unhealthy academic life is. You know, all that reading and writing while you're sitting down. It can't be good for you.'

'Ye-es,' said Ethel, wary of where this was going.

'Yes,' Murdo continued. 'Even the academics agree with me about this. I spoke to Tennyson about it – you know, that old fool from English. He leant me this book.'

Murdo went to his desk and came back with an ancient-looking volume called – he showed Ethel the title – *The Anatomy of Melancholy*, by Robert Burton.

'Let me read you a couple of bits. It's a bit Ye Olde Englishy, but some of this stuff's hilarious.'

'Sure,' said Ethel. Murdo was full of surprises.

'Okay. This is a chapter called "Love of Learning, or overmuch Study. With a Digression of the Misery of Scholars, and why the Muses are Melancholy." Hell of a title. Anyway, this Burton bloke quotes this other guy, Machiavelli, who's talking about scholars: "study weakens their bodies, dulls the spirits, abates their strength and courage, and in general undermines the manlier, martial virtues." Sounds right to me.'

'Some truth to it,' said Ethel, although the general tenor of this was ominous.

'Absolutely. Here's another couple of bits about scholars: they "live a sedentary, solitary life" that is "free from bodily exercise, and those ordinary disports which other men use." See, he's talking about sports there. This is spot-on. People who play sport are healthier; without enough sport, you get ill. So, he says that people who spend their whole time thinking and not exercising are asking for trouble. Thinking "dries the brain and extinguisheth natural heat." All right, I'm not sure what he means by "natural heat", but drying the brain doesn't sound good, does it?'

'It doesn't.' Still ominous.

'And finally, he says, "hard students are commonly troubled with gouts, catarrhs, rheums, cachexi, bradypepsia, bad eyes, stone and colic, crudities, oppilations, vertigo, winds, consumptions, and all such diseases as come by overmuch sitting." Again, not sure what some of those things are, or how to pronounce them, but they don't sound too flash.'

'They don't.'

'I'm sorry to lay all this heavy scholarship on you, Ethel. I know it's not your thing.' Ethel winced. 'But I want you to see where I'm coming from, because we need to do something about this.'

Ethel's sense of alarm was increasing. Was Murdo going to outlaw reading and writing? Even for Leichardt, that might be a step too far.

'Ethel, we've got to get the academic staff to do more exercise. It's for their own good, but more importantly it's for the good of the University. If the workforce is healthier, it will be more productive. Fewer sick days lost for a start.'

'That's hard to argue with,' said Ethel, although she wished she could. She had last exercised about a decade ago.

'But there's a problem,' said Murdo. Thank God, thought Ethel. 'Exercising takes time. And if we're talking about exercise in the workplace, where we can keep tabs on people, that's time taken away from work, isn't it? During work hours, we need the staff to be at work: teaching or applying for grants, or whatever. Work has to take priority. So, it looks as though we can't have exercise as well, doesn't it?'

'Yes, I suppose that's right,' said Ethel, trying to sound disappointed.

'Wrong!'

Murdo got up from the table and fetched something from a corner of the room. At first sight Ethel thought it was some kind of large toaster – its main body was about that size. But then she noticed a pair of pedals sprouting from each side, and what looked like two handles attached to the thing by cables.

'Ethel, I present the Lance Armstrong Portable Underdesk Leg and Arm Exerciser. I got a great deal on these because people have gone off that brand. Personally, I think Lance was misunderstood, but that's another story.'

Unusually for her, Ethel was speechless, squinting suspiciously at the contraption as if it might be an unexploded bomb. Murdo could see her fear and puzzlement.

'It's desk exercise equipment,' he explained. 'The idea is that the staff will be able to exercise while they are working at their desks. Isn't that fantastic? The troops will keep themselves fit without pausing for so much as an instant from their search for external grants. Their enhanced fitness will, in turn, enable them to continue to do that forever – or at any rate until retirement or retrenchment, whichever comes first. What do you think?'

Ethel had to think quickly. 'Murdo, it's a great idea in principle, but …'

'But?'

'But aren't these things already available in the gym?'

'No, they're not, Ethel.' Really, the woman was a bit slow on the uptake. 'The gym has exercise machines, sure, but you have to go to the gym to use them. You can use the Lance Armstrong while you're working at your desk. That's the whole point.'

'Oh, I see,' said Ethel, trying desperately to suppress feelings of horror.

'You still seem underwhelmed,' said Murdo, famous for his knowledge of people, especially their weaknesses.

'Well ...' Ethel cast about for something to cling to in this crisis. And then she had it: 'It's a brilliant idea, Murdo, but I wonder if it's appropriate for senior management.'

'Such as yourself?'

Ethel wasn't going to be caught out as easily as that. 'Yes but you too. Senior managers have such brutal demands on their time. And so many meetings to attend where it wouldn't be practicable to use the equipment. I wonder if it wouldn't be wise to make an exception for senior managers – say, at the level of executive dean and above.'

Fixing Ethel with his protuberant stare, Murdo had to suppress an expression of intense distaste. If there was ever anyone who needed several hours a day on the Lance Armstrong, it was this fat cow. He could see no reason why use of the equipment wouldn't be as practicable for Ethel as for anyone else. It would be fun to see her peddling away during a meeting. However, he had to be careful about this – 'strategic' was the university word. He needed Humpty-Dumpty here as an ally, not an opponent.

'Yeah, I see your point,' he said reluctantly. 'Okay, for senior management the use of the equipment can be voluntary.'

'Thank you, Murdo,' said Ethel.

'But for everyone else we'll mandate a certain period every day – say, an hour to begin with, although I think that's a bit brief – when they have to exercise on the machine. Or maybe they'll have to cover a particular distance or burn a minimum number of calories. I'll have to work on those finer points.'

'Excellent idea,' said Ethel. 'But how will you make sure that the staff who do have to use the equipment will actually use it? What's to stop them saying they have but lying?'

'No problem at all. These things come with a built-in monitor that records time, speed, distance and calories.'

'Aha,' said Ethel, warming to a machine with its own in-built surveillance capability.

'Of course,' said Murdo, 'we'll need to assign some people to go round and check the readings on the monitors – like meter-readers.'

'Okay, but that's a lot of work.'

'Not really, because there's no need to monitor everyone all the time. Every day the exercise monitoring unit can check up on just a few people chosen at random. The staff won't know when they might be monitored. So, if they know what's good for them, they'll police themselves.'

'What if they simply don't comply?'

'Yes, I was coming to that,' said Murdo. 'I thought first of offering workload points as an incentive, but that would undermine the principle that this is exercise you need to perform while you're working, not instead of it.'

'Yes, of course.'

'So, it would be better to use a system of sticks rather than carrots, I reckon. In fact, the system I have in mind is essentially the same as the one we've just agreed on for the policing of the corporate look using small courses. Anyone found to be desk-exercise non-compliant could be docked a suitable number of workload points. They'll have to make those points up somehow, and the executive dean can decide how. In other words, if they don't exercise, we can allocate punitive work assignments of various kinds – extra teaching, tutoring, marking, admin. Maybe painting rocks in the carpark.'

Ethel thrilled to the word 'punitive.' 'Terrific! But of course, there'll always be a few recalcitrants who won't comply in spite of everything.'

'There are always bastards like that. But again, no problem. Those people we simply get rid of.' Smiling broadly, Murdo made a throat-slitting gesture.

'Yes!' Ethel could imagine various wasters being made to walk the plank.

'In fact, that reminds me of one last thing I wanted to ask,' said Murdo. 'I've been working on a list of staff members whose aspirations no longer align with those of the University.' That phrase had felt awkward at first but was now tripping off the tongue nicely. 'There are quite a few names on the list now, but I wondered if you had any to add?'

'I'm sure I can think of a few.'

'From your College I was thinking of Bruno Whelper. He seems to do hardly any research – not many publications or grants. Few runs on the board for years.'

'That's true,' said Ethel, 'Whelper's research output is paltry – and his input is worse. However, I don't recommend adding him to the list because he's a big supporter of senior management. Whenever he's in the presence of someone with power, he comes over all tingly. He absolutely loves you, for example.'

'Ah, now you mention it, I think I saw that myself when I visited that tribe of drop-kicks in Social Studies. He was practically groveling. All right, Whelper sounds more valuable than I thought. Can you suggest anyone else?'

'Oh, yes. I'll send you a full list, but I can mention one person straight away: Geoff Medway. I thought he was all right, but he's turned out to be disloyal to me, opposed to Target 1%, and a non-performer in grants. Also, Whelper tells me that he wrote a rude poem about you which he read out in public.'

'Medway, of course. No worries, Ethel, he's already on the list.'

13

CLIMATE CHANGE

Medway, back in the ranks, returned to a working schedule similar to his old routine before he became a school dean, a steady diet of teaching – lectures, tutorials and seminars – and low-level admin related to teaching, with occasional desultory attempts to get on with some research. But there were differences too.

As usual, he would begin the day by checking his email, but while he was doing that he would now be peddling away on his Lance Armstrong underdesk exerciser. He'd thought about joining the resistance against this latest outrage but was afraid his situation was too vulnerable for that to be a good idea. His fear originated from the following email.

Dear teammates,

As you know, we're pursuing Target 1%. Today I announce two major initiatives that will assist us in achieving that goal.

First, it's a source of great concern to me that many staff members are not as physically fit as they should be. To remedy this, all staff members (other than senior management) will henceforth be required to spend one hour per day working out on desk exercise equipment. Compliance will be monitored, and noncompliance will be penalised by deduction of workload points. Further details will follow shortly.

Second, I'm sorry to say that not everyone is complying with the University's corporate look policy. While many people are, and I thank them for their support, others are still giving classes and appearing at other university events in non-corporate attire. This is deeply disappointing and lets the side down. It's not how we thrashed the Poms three times in a row under my leadership!

I am therefore introducing measures to encourage compliance with the corporate look principal.

From now on, there will be no online recording or streaming of any lecture or other event unless the presenter is wearing a Leichardt blazer. During hot weather a Make Leichardt Great T-shirt will be okay. The Make Leichardt Great cap is optional but strongly recommended.

Best regards,
Murdo
Professor Murdo McMurdo
President and Vice-Chancellor

Medway had to read the email three times to absorb its full import. The first time, he was distracted by the misspelling of the word 'principle', which was a frequent feature of messages from the central administration at all levels. The second time, he was too busy marvelling at the whole notion of Target 1% and the corporate look to take in what Murdo was saying in addition. Only at the third reading did Medway begin to understand what was being said, and its implications for his own case.

If he didn't exercise on the Lance Armstrong and wear the wretched uniform, he'd lose workload points that he couldn't afford to lose. He already had small course problems even without Murdo's proclamation. The first-year course that he co-taught with Nick was doing well but his two upper-year courses were in major difficulties. Twenty years earlier, they had about seventy enrolments each. Over the years this fell to fifty, then to thirty, finally to fifteen or less.

How had this happened? A series of administrative reforms had played their part, but Medway also had to acknowledge his own negligence. For years, he had seen these problems gathering pace but his attempts to address them were intermittent and ineffective. Most of his energies went into research, teaching, and Faculty- or School-level administration. When he became dean, he could have used his position to shore things up, but he regarded this as beneath the dignity of his office. He was also too preoccupied trying to plug up the numerous holes in the leaky dyke of Social Work. The securing of his own teaching seemed a low priority.

But Medway's teaching was now an urgent priority – for him, at any rate. Deaning had been a full-time job, and he had done little teaching for the past year. Suddenly, he needed to get his teaching moving again in order to meet his targets under the workload plan. No special allowance would be made for post-dean recovery.

The upshot was that, at the start of each new semester, it was touch and go whether any of Medway's upper-year courses would run. The current small-course threshold for upper-year courses was fifteen, and that was the approximate enrolment he was getting for these classes now. His entreaties to the effect that, 'small' or not, his upper-year courses were essential to a proper education in politics or public policy impressed no one but himself. All that mattered were the numbers, and behind them the money. As a consequence, his upper-year courses sometimes ran and sometimes were cancelled at the last moment. Any cancellation could lead to his being asked to take on disagreeable tasks in order to meet his workload targets.

So, Murdo's fiat left Medway with little choice. He needed to don the blazer to have even a fifty-fifty chance of teaching his upper-year classes, and he had to exercise to keep whatever points he managed to get. In both cases, the alternative was to invite the kind of arbitrary punishment of which Ethel was a supreme exponent.

With profound feelings of nausea and humiliation, he kept pedalling and sent in his measurements for a Leichardt blazer and Make Leichardt Great T-shirt.

***

It did him no good. One morning, with a week to go before a new semester started, the phone rang.

'Hi Geoff,' whined an unpleasant nasal voice with an English accent of indeterminate origin.

It was Ethel's flunkey, Dicky Sediment, the dean of Human Instruments. Medway was aware of him in part because of Sediment's pointless thwarting of Beadle's willingness to supervise graduate research. There were also communications to the academic staff in which Sediment had decreed various cost-saving measures, such as increasing the minimum number of students in first-year tutorials from fifteen to eighteen, then twenty-two. Presumably, this was what was meant by being 'student-centred.' Medway could imagine Sediment advising Ethel on how to pack more victims into the Black Hole of Calcutta.

'We're trying to work out the teaching arrangements for the coming semester,' said Sediment. 'I'm sorry, but your upper-year course in political theory has to be cancelled under the small courses rule.' The chances of Sediment's being sorry about this, or about anything that caused problems for others, were remote.

'That's disappointing,' said Medway. Even the blazer hadn't saved him. He'd signed a written undertaking to wear one, so his course was listed as recorded online, but apparently he still didn't have sufficient enrolments for the class to run. His grovelling submission to the moloch of Murdo's program had not been enough.

'We'd like you to do something else instead.' Christ, here it comes, thought Medway. Was it in *Bonfire of the Vanities* that Tom Wolfe refers to 'the snout of the beast' breaking the surface?

'Yes, what's that?'

'We've discovered that Pleonexia is seriously overloaded.' The snout – or should it be beak? – was visible. One of Pleonexia's many skills was the ability to lighten her own workload by dumping parts of it onto unwary colleagues. Past victims included Nick and (less unjustly) Whelper.

'Really? I calculated her workload when I was dean and it was normal.'

'She's taken on increased amounts of work since then, and they push her well over the limit. So, it's a priority now to get Pleonexia's workload back under control.'

What were the increased amounts of work Pleonexia was doing? And what about the priority of letting Medway teach his subject? But it was obvious where this was heading.

Sure enough. 'We want you to take over Pleonexia's course, *The Politics of Climate Change*.'

'My God, I know nothing about climate change. And teaching starts next week.'

'Yes, we know it's a bit tight, but we have no choice.' A bit tight? You have no choice?

Fortunately, Pleonexia had organised the course to minimise her own teaching duties, and Medway benefited from this too. Most of the lectures were done by guest lecturers, and most of the tutorials, or 'workshops' (should hammers and chisels be issued?), consisted of presentations by the students. Some of these had an entertainingly comical quality, like very bad stand-up.

Still, just to be able to preside over it all, Medway needed to swot up a lot of climate change literature in a hurry. All he knew about the issue was what everyone knew who read the newspapers or watched the television news. As can be imagined, there was a mountain of academic work that went well beyond this. Medway began with Anthony Giddens, *The Politics of Climate Change* (2009), and went on from there. Reading some of this was no bad thing in itself, since it was new and interesting to him, but in order to get it done in the time not available, he had to put aside almost everything else, including all his own research, for a couple of months.

When he saw the class list, Medway could see why the College wanted him to teach *Climate Change* rather than something he actually knew about. Pleonexia's class had no more enrolments than his own but there was an important difference: they were international students. There were one or two Australians, usually public servants trying to improve their qualifications, but most were from China, Indonesia, India, Bangladesh, Nepal, Papua New Guinea and other places. As mentioned earlier, the thing about international students was that, unlike the locals, they were full-fee-paying, hence highly sought after by the University. Indeed, universities all over the globe were now in furious competition to attract more international students to make up for the lack of public funding experienced everywhere. Medway thus found himself at the cutting edge – or should it be the front box-office? – of the modern university.

Teaching international students did have its advantages, and these were on display as soon as Medway entered the room to teach his first class of *Climate Change*.

'Good morning!' he said as brightly as he could.

'Good morning!' the students chorused back to him. If they'd been locals, they would have responded with a wary, sullen or distracted silence while engrossed in their mobile phones. The international students, by contrast, always gave the impression that they could not wait to ingest whatever sustenance he cared to cast their way. They were attentive, industrious, polite, and deferential. They almost always addressed Medway as 'Professor.'

But he was also ambivalent about the international students, as he was about so many things at Leichardt. Their English-language levels were extremely variable and some of them could hardly speak a word. Their written work could be diabolical. Mercifully, Medway did not have to know too much about the details of their research. This was just as well because, in addition to *Climate Change*, Medway was put in charge of the Masters-level research dissertation course. There he discovered that each of the students had their own specialist supervisor for their individual projects, which usually dealt with matters such as 'Nepalese Social Security' and 'Solid Waste Management in Jakarta,' about which Medway knew nothing and did not care to know much more.

On the whole, teaching the research course was not difficult. Medway just had to co-ordinate proceedings, give a few introductory seminars about how to design and structure a research dissertation, get the dissertations examined and calculate the marks. Nor, however, was it the kind of teaching he'd signed up for at the start of his career. Back then he'd had a strong sense of helping to transmit a culture. No doubt the story of Western thought was contestable – *should* be contested – but at least there was a field which the students were sufficiently engaged with to contest. It was their story. The international students, although personally delightful, came to Leichardt at best as disinterested anthropologists observing from the outside such alien preoccupations as human rights, personal liberty and democracy, and more often as utilitarian careerists who would rote-learn whatever was necessary to get better jobs. Critical thinking about political ideas was, for many of them, like landing on the moon.

***

There was a knock on the door – timid, tentative, a signal from someone who wished to remain anonymous.

'Come in,' said Medway. Nothing happened.

'Come in!' said Medway, raising his voice. Still nothing. He got up from his desk and opened the door. There in the corridor was a female student. She had reddish-brown hair, a face full of freckles, and prominent front teeth.

'Hi,' said the student, 'I'm Shirley.'

'Ah yes,' said Medway. 'Please come in and have at seat at the table.' Shirley shuffled in, her eyes downcast, and sat.

'Thanks for coming in,' said Medway. 'Now, I'm afraid we have to deal with this allegation that you've violated the rules of academic integrity.'

Alas, it was true. As the semester wore on, Medway had become Academic Integrity Officer for the Government section of the College. He had sworn off further leadership roles while Ethel was still in control, but he had to do some administration and this was all that was on offer. Most of the routine academic integrity matters were dealt with by the relevant lecturer, but the more serious or difficult cases of plagiarism and other dishonesty were passed to Medway. There was also an integrity officer higher up the chain at college level (so much for eliminating levels of administration). It was a tedious job but Medway had done many things like this before.

'Okay,' said Medway. 'Now, Nick Wedgwood-Benn alleges that in your first-year exam in *Introduction to Modern Ideologies* you cheated by bringing into the exam notes written on your wrist and the palm of your hand.'

'No, I didn't,' said Shirley.

'Well, the exam invigilators have sent me these photos which clearly show that your palm and wrist are covered in notes. Here, have a look.' Medway passed the photos across and Shirley studied them carefully.

'Yeah, all right, I did the notes,' said Shirley. 'But I did them during the exam.'

'Really? You're saying you didn't bring the notes into the exam with you. Rather, you wrote them while you were sitting the exam. Is that right?'

'Yeah.'

'But why did you do that? In the exam you're given an exam booklet for writing your answers in, and you're given scribbling paper to make any notes on. Why didn't you write your notes on the scribbling paper?'

'I didn't want to.'

'Why not?'

'I was following Fucko's advice.'

'Fucko?'

'Yeah, Fucko, the French guy.'

Medway had to think for a moment. 'You don't mean Foucault, do you?'

'Yeah, him: Fucko.' Bullseye! Michel strikes again, thought Medway.

'Okay, so how is Fucko – I mean, Foucault – relevant?'

'Fucko says that "social reality is inscribed on the body." Here, I'll show you the reading.' Shirley rummaged in her bag, extracted a tattered Sociology reader and passed it to Medway, pointing to a passage about postmodernism and Foucault. The passage was decorated with lurid pink highlighting along with some underlining and the comment 'COOL!!!' Sure enough, it referred to social reality being inscribed on the body.

'Jesus,' Medway muttered involuntarily.

'Sorry?'

'I mean, yes, I see.'

'So, I was just following the advice of Fucko. He says to inscribe on the body.'

Medway was about to distinguish between advising and describing, but saw that this might commit him to explaining Foucault again, and thought better of it.

'So he does,' said Medway. 'All right, Shirley, let's call this a misunderstanding. By all means continue to inscribe reality on your body, but when it comes to exams, next time please just write your notes on the scribble paper. Okay?'

'Okay. Thanks for your time.'

'You're welcome. Goodbye.'

14

SPHAGNUM'S COCKROACH

'You know, you don't have to be there,' said Sarah.

'Another couple of years, maybe, not long. I just want to get to my superannuation savings target,' said Medway.

'It's not worth it if it's making you sick.'

'It's somewhat sickening, but I'm surviving.'

'Only just. It distresses me to see you like this. That woman is appalling. She reminds me of my last principal. And as for Murdo, what a disgusting individual.'

'I know. Not much longer …' Medway kissed Sarah and left for work.

***

He was indeed unwell. It began as a stubborn pain behind his nose. At first he thought it was cold-related, but it wouldn't go away. He went to see his GP, Dr Fred Sphagnum, one of the doctors at the Leichardt Health Centre in the Client Services Building. With a massive head and bushy beard, Sphagnum looked like one of the monuments on Easter Island carved to resemble Brian Blessed. For some reason he wore shorts in all seasons, as if he'd just come from doing his own building or plumbing at home. This was in keeping with his practical, no-nonsense approach to medical practice. Perhaps he was really a tradie, as Winter had pretended to be and Owen was now, and just offered medical advice as a sideline.

Sphagnum also had a wry sense of humour and seemed to enjoy Medway's accounts of the latest outrages up the hill, which were apparently of a piece with his own experiences of the University. He was especially entertained by Murdo's drive to raise Leichardt to the top 1% of universities. After taking Medway's blood pressure and finding that it was on the high side, he cheerfully announced that Leichardt was already 'in the top 1% of blood pressure-increasing universities.'

Medway's pain got worse. After further tests, Sphagnum diagnosed 'trigeminal facial neuralgia.' Over the coming months Medway's symptoms developed into a chronic pattern in which episodes of massive pain would migrate around several locations on the right side of his face. Over the course of weeks at a time, the site of the pain would start at the corner of his mouth, move to the tip of his nose, travel up his nose into his eye socket, then radiate into his temple. The pain was not there all the time but would be set off by the slightest touch. Eating, brushing his teeth or showering could be agony. After several months like this, the condition would ease off and disappear. Then it would come back again later.

There was no telling how long the bad spell would last or whether it would ever end.

The pain had a distinctly electrical quality, so that when it was in progress Medway felt as though someone – Murdo or Ethel, perhaps – had hooked him up to a battery of electrodes and flicked the switch. This sense of being electrocuted was caused by the pain's location in the nervous system. Medway eventually learned that the problem originated in damage to the large trigeminal nerve that runs down the centre of the head. The image he formed, rightly or wrongly, was of something like frayed nerve-endings waving about inside his skull and coming into contact with other parts with which they had no business coming into contact.

His own online research yielded such cheering tidbits as the fact that the condition was known colloquially as a 'suicide disease' because many of its sufferers had opted to remove themselves from the planet. Fortunately, not all instances were that bad; Medway's could be debilitating and depressing but he never got to the stage of 'to be or not to be.' It was nevertheless extremely distressing, and it was little comfort to learn that the disorder had had a distinguished philosophical sufferer in C. S. Peirce, the nineteenth-century American pragmatist. If that was the price of philosophy, Medway was willing never to think again.

Sphagnum could not confirm that Medway's neuralgia was definitely due to stress, but he thought it more than likely. Its first signs had coincided with the arrival of Ethel. Flareups since then could be aligned with other Ethel-related horrors.

Whatever the cause, the available treatment was pretty limited. According to Sphagnum, there was 'no cure, only management' – a phrase that, it occurred to Medway, could rival 'show me the money' as an appropriate motto for Leichardt. Management of Medway's neuralgia consisted in taking the kind of drugs often used to treat epilepsy: nerve-calming pills that did the job up to a point – they at least took the edge off the worst of the pain – but at the price of periods of almost unbearable drowsiness. If he took more than one pill at a time, he became so dizzy that he could not walk in a straight line. Perhaps he would soon be fast asleep during seminars, head lolling and mouth open, like his old friend Dwight DeLillo, who had kept everyone entertained in the days of the old Politics department.

It did make it harder for Medway to do his job. Usually he could function tolerably well, but sometimes the pain from the electrical vibrations in his head made it hard to project his voice in lectures. At its worst he found it difficult even to hold a one-to-one conversation – it was completely impossible to join in the traditional shouting competition with Millicent. His general situation reminded him of a line from Joni Mitchell's 'Furry sings the Blues': 'It's mostly muttering now and sideshow spiel.'

Still, Sphagnum was reassuring about the future. 'Don't worry,' he said, 'we'll survive all this. You and I are like cockroaches.' By 'all this', Sphagnum meant not only Medway's neuralgia but the whole world of Leichardt. It occurred to Medway that his experience with Ethel was indeed like that of Gregor Samsa, waking one morning, 'after a night of uneasy dreams,' to find himself transformed into a giant insect. It was a worry that Kafka's human insect is subsequently tormented to death. Medway could imagine Ethel opening the door to his room and prodding him with a stick, aiming for his soft underbelly. But there was also something pleasing about Sphagnum's cockroach image. Medway could see Sphagnum and himself subsisting deep in the woodwork of the institution, their presence viscerally offensive to its proprietors, who could torment but not eradicate them.

Medway did think about taking some extended sick leave. This would be a new departure for him: in more than twenty years at Leichardt he had never taken any sick leave at all. The polar opposite in this respect of Nigel Plume, who was rarely seen on campus because of various health issues, Medway had never missed a single lecture, tutorial or meeting of any kind because of illness, even though there were many times when he felt less than chipper. Looking back on this record, he wondered why he had bothered. What prize did he think he was going to win for this display of stoicism? Indeed, he learned from the University's website that this kind of behaviour was now frowned upon as amounting to the vice of 'presenteeism', the opposite of absenteeism and just as blameworthy. Apparently, it was Plume, not Medway, who had been following University policy.

Nevertheless, he decided against taking sick leave. The University's rules said that this would be possible only for half a year or so before the situation would need to be reviewed. Then what? If he said he could not do his job, he might be invited to leave. On the whole, he thought he could manage with the help of Sphagnum's pills, and that it would be best to soldier on as he was for the time being.

To keep his spirits up, he composed a brief ditty to sing in the car on the way to work. It was set to the tune of *Skippy*.

> Leichardt, Leichardt,
> Leichardt, the uni on the hill,
> Leichardt, Leichardt,
> Leichardt, it makes you very ill.

***

His mood was not improved by another announcement from Murdo.

Dear Teammates,

I wish to give notice of an important initiative. From next Monday no one will be served at any commercial outlet on campus unless they are wearing at least one item of official merchandise – either the Leichardt blazer or the Make Leichardt Great T-shirt or cap. I'm sure everyone who is serious about playing on the Leichardt team will appreciate the wisdom and necessity of this move.

Kind regards,
Murdo
Professor Murdo McMurdo
President, Vice-Chancellor, and Skipper

No sooner had he absorbed this latest abomination than Medway received a visit from Pleonexia Self.

'Ethel wanted me to let you know,' she said with a smile, 'that another political theory professor is being appointed.'

Pleonexia handed Medway the photocopied CV of a 'Professor Fernando Obscurando.'

'Good grief,' said Medway, 'where has this come from?'

'Ethel says it's not her idea. It's come from Murdo. Fernando is part of a spousal package Murdo has accepted so he can bring in Fernando's wife, Eva Fledermaus, as executive dean of the College of Social Control.'

'So, Fernando is part of her luggage?'

'Yes, they're a Foucauldian power couple – both experts on Foucault and other continental stuff.' It never ceased to amaze Medway how people who professed various radical political positions – Marxism, Maoism, Foucauldian postmodernism – were also happy to operate the oppressive system they said they opposed if that advanced their careers. Although, in this case that was immediately true only of Fledermaus, not Obscurando, who was only an indirect beneficiary of Fledermaus's complicity. Glancing at his CV, Medway saw that his particular specialty was the work of Hans Fimmel the famous historical sociologist. Fimmel had visited Leichardt early in Medway's time, and his seminar had been – to understate the matter by some distance – hard to follow.

'I see,' said Medway. From the perspective of his self-interest, a worrying aspect of Obscurando's arrival was that there was now an additional political theorist when the numbers of upper-year undergraduates doing political theory were declining to vanishing point. There were scarcely enough local students for Medway to graze on, let alone with competition from someone else. Might the presence of Obscurando be used as leverage against him?

As if anticipating his thoughts, Pleonexia said, 'Ethel wanted me to assure you that this is not aimed at you. Obscurando has been imposed on her by Murdo, but she doesn't see his arrival as a threat to your position.' This was followed by an artificial smile that made it perfectly clear that Pleonexia didn't believe Ethel's assurance and that Ethel didn't believe it either.

'That's reassuring,' said Medway in the same vein of irony. 'I keep hearing rumours that Murdo has a hit list.'

'Oh, there's a hit list,' said Pleonexia with satisfaction.

'How do you know? Have you seen it?'

'No, but my friend Betty has.'

'How did she get to see … never mind, I'll take your word for it.' Medway would never take Pleonexia's word for anything.

'I'm sure it exists.'

'Sure,' said Medway. 'But on the subject of Obscurando again, does Ethel have any comment on the ethics of appointing someone to a scarce professorial post just because he's married to someone else?' When Medway had been a dean, some pressure had been placed on him to support a similar proposal, which would have lumbered the School with a mediocre sociologist so that the university could get a scientist it wanted. Medway refused to have anything to do with it. But in Obscurando's case, there seemed to be no choice (so Ethel said); Murdo had simply decreed that he would join them.

'Ethel didn't say anything about that,' said Pleonexia. 'But I think that spousal packages can be defended from a feminist point of view. The spouse who's being headhunted is usually the male, so without the spousal package it's the female who tends to suffer.'

'Not in this case.'

'Not in this case, no. But the general principle is defensible.'

'I'm not sure I agree. But as usual, that scarcely matters, does it? The decision has been made and there's nothing I or anyone can do about it.'

'I'm afraid that's true,' said Pleonexia, trying and failing to project an impression of empathy.

After Pleonexia had left, Medway looked up one of Obscurando's articles. The abstract told him all he needed to know.

This essay unpacks Hans Fimmel's account of civilisation. It argues that the problematic of civilisation constitutes the needle's eye through which Fimmel's intellectual odyssey must be seen, his recent turn to foreground the interplay of culture and power (as the religio-political nexus) notwithstanding. Fimmel's approach to civilisation is foundational to his illumination of the human condition, which is illuminated here as the interaction of a historical cultural hermeneutics and a macro-phenomenology of the world as a shared horizon. The essay discusses Fimmel's articulation of his account of civilisation as a contribution to the elucidation of the 'meaning of meaning.' It argues that Fimmel's theory of civilisation penetrates beyond socio-centric perspectives, and, in so doing, offers a critique of what might be called sociological solipsism, or historical auto-eroticism. In decentring society/anthropos, a more nuanced understanding of the human condition as a unity in diversity, or maybe a diverse holism, is achieved.

Medway had to take his hat off to one of the most loathsome pieces of writing he had ever come across – even in academia, which was saying something. How had Obscurando managed to cram so much awfulness into such a relatively short passage? The man had talent, it couldn't be denied. There was the jargon, of course: 'religio-political nexus', 'historical cultural hermeneutics', 'macro-phenomenology', and the rest. There were the cliches: 'unpacks' (Medway recalled one of his own lecturers, Knud Jurgensson, warning him against this word forty years before: 'Too many things are being unpacked these days,' Knud had said. 'I wish they were packed up again.'), 'the problematic' (a pompous adjective masquerading as an even more pompous noun, meaning only a big problem or set of problems), and so on. There was the unintended comedy of a problematic that 'constitutes the needle's eye' through which an 'odyssey' takes place (Odysseus had enough problems, or problematics, without this), and of 'a unity in diversity, or maybe a diverse holism.' But the biggest difficulty of all with the passage was, what the hell – no, what the Fucko – did it mean? Frankly, thought Medway, life is too short to try to find out.

Obscurando, when he arrived, turned out to be a lovely man, friendly and outgoing. He got in touch with Medway and they met for coffee. Coffee itself proved to be unobtainable, the two professors being refused service because neither was, at the time, wearing the appropriate corporate attire. They retreated to Medway's room to chat anyway, and Obscurando soon demonstrated that he was as incomprehensible in person as in his published writing. It remained to be seen whether his presence would be used against Medway by Ethel. Her assurance to the contrary was itself a bad sign.

***

But there were good signs too. One resulted from the retirement of Fido Inkster. Medway had counselled him to wait for the coming academic restructure, which might enable him to claim a voluntary redundancy payout. However, Fido was advised by Sediment that the restructure could be a long way off and that if he wanted to leave he should go now. This struck Medway as an outcome much more convenient for the College than for Fido. But Fido, with his unerring instinct for acting against his own interests, chose to go nonetheless.

Medway assumed that, in keeping with tradition, there would be some kind of farewell function for Fido, and when nothing was forthcoming from the discipline's ostensible leaders, he asked them about it. Plume said he was too ill, and Pleonexia said it was Plume's job. They suggested that, if Medway was so keen to give Fido a send-off, he might like to organise it himself. This he did, although with the background thought that things had degenerated when the so-called leaders couldn't be arsed to do what was patently their duty. At a small lunch gathering in the pretentious new University restaurant in the Client Services Building overlooking CHQ, Medway made a brief speech to the effect that Fido was one of a dying breed of academic who cared about scholarship for its own sake, and that it was regrettable that the contemporary university seemed to have no place for such a person. Beadle was present and did not disagree.

Fido's departure meant that his courses in the Graduate Program had to be taught by someone else. Medway had his eye on Fido's *Ethics and Public Administration* course, which would enable him to teach several ethical theories he was familiar with and then broaden his range by studying some of their practical applications in public policy and administration. He let his interest be known and was given the green light to take the course over.

The upshot was that, although Medway's teaching platform was increasingly utilitarian, driven by demand from full-fee paying international students, it was also increasingly secure. The upper-year undergraduate courses were collapsing and would soon be discontinued. But just as that ship was disappearing beneath the waves, he had come across the life raft of the Graduate Program, with its legions of international students, in which he could teach three different courses, all of them part of the required core of the Program. He would no longer be vulnerable to having Pleonexia's cast-offs imposed upon him. His teaching future appeared assured.

***

Another good thing happened. An email arrived from the Academy of Social Sciences in Australia, which began,

> Dear Professor Medway,
>
> I have great pleasure in informing you that you have been elected to a fellowship of the Academy.

In the context of Australian academia, this was like being elevated to the House of Lords. He was entitled to place the letters, 'FASSA', after his name. This gave him the same academic status (although not the same money) as the Leichardt Distinguished Professors. Like them, he was surely now untouchable.

The process had begun earlier in the year when the School of Social Studies had still been in existence and Medway had still been its dean. Into his office one afternoon bustled Bruce Whitelist, a short, stout man with thick, curly silver hair. He was the School's Strategic Professor, charged with stimulating research performance by putting the staff in touch people in the state government and local industry. His method for doing this was to host a series of lunches downtown, which from all reports rivalled supper with Trimalchio, Babette's feast and *La Grande Bouffe*. He was well placed to do this, having an extraordinary network of contacts as a result of high-level service in the state government and later at the Australian National University. Whitelist was as well connected as it was possible to be in Australia, short of being a media personality, resources tycoon, or sports celebrity like Murdo. Among his affiliations was a long-standing fellowship of the Academy. He now proposed to nominate Medway, arguing that this would be good for him and good for Leichardt. Whitelist thought that Medway had a sufficient track record in research and publication for this to be possible.

Medway was at first taken aback, never having considered such a thing before, and being scarcely aware of the Academy's existence. But he could see no reason not to try, and gave his permission for Whitelist to proceed. Whitelist found seconders for the nomination, and sent it in. Weeks had passed and Medway had almost forgotten about it, but suddenly he was a Fellow of the Academy.

Whitelist made sure the news was announced on the University's website, and Medway began to receive messages of congratulations from all over Leichardt. Friends and colleagues emailed or phoned or called in on him. He had a rare email from Sediment. He even heard from the University's Deputy Vice-Chancellor (Research), Ron Santos, and took the opportunity to point out that although he was now an academician, he would not be able to meet the University research expectations that Santos had instituted. Santos replied vaguely that he was sure 'something could be worked out' in Medway's college. Obviously he was unaware that the college's head was Ethel. Indeed, Ethel was a notable omission from the list of Medway's well-wishers. Her silence was, it seemed to him, one of her more eloquent communications.

Medway and Sarah went to Canberra for his induction, along with the rest of that year's draft, at the Academy's annual meeting. The event took place over two days at a strange, dome-shaped auditorium that might have been designed by Buckminster Fuller in the 1970s, located near the Academy's headquarters on the outskirts of the Australian National University. Almost everyone stayed in the same university hotel nearby.

The first session on the agenda was the presentation of the new Fellows, at which they all had to summarise their research in three-minute presentations. Leichardt had recently taken to inflicting a 'three-minute thesis' competition on its research students, challenging them to explain within that fleeting timeframe what their work was about. Medway had thought this was an excellent idea, but now it was his turn to try to explain himself instantly. In his case the three minutes had to accommodate thirty years of work – a task akin to Fimmel's odyssey through the needle's eye. He managed, but it wasn't easy. The strain of concentrating on his lines and not going over time, together with tinkling background notes of neuralgia, made it feel as though he was undergoing a form of torture. A video of the event recorded the agonised expression on his face for posterity.

On the second day there were meetings and addresses, followed by the dinner where the new fellows were to be formally inducted. The place was positively packed with luminaries, many well-known and with AMs, AOs and ACs after their names. Sarah and Medway sat at a table with some philosophers and sociologists, including Kate Cardigan. One of the philosophers had been at Oxford around the same time Medway was there; another was a theorist of international relations who knew Owen. Halfway through the evening, the new fellows filed up to the stage and received their certificates and badges.

It was all very grand, but what Medway liked most about it was the sense of being part of a community that actually cared about academic inquiry as something good in itself. Here were university people who were less interested in racking up large sums in external grants (although some of them had no doubt done that) than in doing research that would get at the truth and benefit people. Amazing. Medway felt that the tawdry world of Leichardt – or, more accurately, what people like Ethel and Murdo had made of Leichardt – was a distant memory.

He could also not help feeling that, when he returned to Leichardt, the Academy fellowship would make him secure against whatever Murdo might have planned. Others might be in difficulty, and he would do what he could for them (probably not much), but his own situation looked secure. His teaching was solid. He was not getting grants, but his publications were recovering. The Academy, surely, had rendered him impregnable. Like Sphagnum's cockroach, he was embedded in the woodwork.

15

CHANGE MANAGEMENT

Target 1% moved to its next phase: Murdo announced that the restructure would be extended to academic posts. Many people would be, in the anodyne language of the bureaucracy, 'affected' – for once the bureaucrats avoided the cant word 'impacted', perhaps because in this case it was too close to the truth. Their posts would be 'discontinued' and replaced by new posts which they would have to apply for if they wished to remain employed. Here, finally, was the moment that Leichardt's academics had been waiting for, and dreading. They had seen the professional staff decimated and the administrative structure turned inside out. Now Murdo was coming for them.

Not everyone would be affected, although in a wider sense everyone was. Some posts were deemed to be 'out of scope' and would continue without change. In some cases whole units would be unmolested – usually in the natural sciences. Elsewhere entire units would be gutted. The senior management of each college would be at liberty to decide where changes needed to be made – or perhaps quotas had been decreed from the centre; as usual it was unclear. At any rate, executive deans like Ethel had an open invitation to eliminate critics and settle old scores.

The goals of the academic restructure were complex and partly concealed. One explicit target was the replacement of many so-called 'balanced' positions, which combined teaching and research, by a new generation of 'teaching specialist' posts. According to Murdo, this was desirable because there were too many people in balanced roles who in fact did little research. Claims were maintained that 50% of Leichardt's balanced staff produced no publications, or hardly any. These claims may have been true a decade earlier, but they were hard to believe now. Who were these people who, after the great publication drive that had been going on for years, still produced nothing?

Medway knew hardly anyone in that category: in Government there were just two cases. One was Whelper, who had given up exerting himself in research and was now cruising, making up for his paucity of outputs (or inputs) with additional teaching. The other was Charlie Putz, a good-natured but inert time-server in international relations. Since his appointment at the turn of the century, Putz had repaid the University's faith by teaching competently and publishing scarcely anything. Ethel had tried to sack him, but he always enlisted the help of the Union and saw her off with the sang-froid of the defenders of Rorke's Drift repelling the Zulus. Apart from Whelper and Putz, all the other noted underperformers in research had either retired or shuffled off permanently. Everyone who remained appeared to be publishing regularly.

Of course, the new research expectations were going to make it possible for the College and University to say that almost all of the staff were failing in research more broadly conceived, since on the new definition 'research' really meant making money. But Murdo's rationale specifically cited publications, and there was little evidence that Medway and most of his companions, or anyone they knew, were doing badly in that respect.

Another goal of the restructure was to 'shake up' and 'rebalance' the staff profile by culling the number of staff at associate professor and above, replacing them with entry-level lecturers. Here is where the unstated goals began to come in – Murdo denied these but no one believed his denials. One was that culling the more senior ranks would enable Murdo to reduce the staffing budget. In addition, by clearing out older, established staff, Murdo would eliminate many people who clung to 'old fashioned' ideas about what a university might stand for. These people were 'not team players.' Murdo could only benefit by having a new cohort of younger academics, grateful to get any job and having no expectations other than trying to meet the new metric-driven targets. For them, it would be the only world they knew.

At a deeper level still, Murdo's scheme was also a piece of creative accountancy. By eliminating so many balanced positions, he would instantly raise Leichardt's research performance overall and consequently Leichardt's position in the world rankings. That was because fewer staff would then count as researchers, and those who remained in this category would be seen to be producing a much higher average of outputs and inputs than when the pool of researchers was larger. Those who were moved into the teaching-only group would be free to produce nothing (or more accurately, whatever research they produced would not be credited towards their workload) and their supposed inactivity would not besmirch the University's research figures.

The result would be the creation of two academic classes. There would be an aristocratic race of researchers, publishing, winning grants and basking in the University's gratitude, and a subservient race of teachers, toiling for the privilege of their existence being tolerated. Most of the aristocrats would be scientists; most of the toilers would be non-scientists. Medway imagined something like the Eloi and Morlocks of H. G. Wells. The humanitarian and social-scientist Eloi would labour in the heat or cold of the elements, hewing full-fee-paying international students out of the dead rock, lashed occasionally by overseers like Ethel. The scientist Morlocks would live bland but opulent, grant-funded lives in airconditioned comfort. When resources tightened, one or two Eloi would be sacrificed to ensure that the system continued.

Murdo denied that his scheme entailed any kind of hierarchy, insisting that the teaching specialists would have the same opportunities for promotion as the researchers. In theory, someone could become a top-level professor by teaching only. No one believed this to be possible in practice, and it did not add up even in theory because the whole premise of the scheme was that it was research that attracted greater kudos to the University. It was obvious that the researchers were going to get the lion's share of whatever recognition was available.

The plan had its ironies. One was that it was teaching, not research, that still accounted for most of the University's income. Another was that most of the University's income from teaching was generated by the humanities and social sciences, since that was where most of the students were enrolled. Nevertheless, the future would belong, more than ever, to research, to research in the form of grant-getting, and therefore to research in the natural sciences. Yet another irony was that the targeting of the senior staff would in effect punish those who had been promoted by the University in the past, hence those who had worked hardest and had the most success.

Murdo's plan proceeded. Each of the colleges would publish its own proposal for change in compliance with Murdo's overall priorities.

The first change proposal, from the College of Optimal Somatic Functioning, set a terrifying precedent. Although the natural sciences could in general expect privileged treatment from Murdo, there were allied areas where people were not so secure in the face of his intentions. One of these was the Nursing unit within Somatic, which did a lot of teaching but not so much research. Suddenly, email inboxes were full of the lamentations of Nursing lecturers whose posts had disappeared to be replaced either by teaching-specialist positions or by nothing. People who had worked solidly and well for the University for over twenty years were tossed onto the 'affected' list. There would be jobs for some, not all of them, and those jobs would often be teaching-specialist, with no recognition of their research.

Those who could not get their job back or transition to Eloi status could opt to be placed on the redeployment list, allowing them to apply for jobs elsewhere in the University. Of course, an academic's chances of being redeployed were slim because academics are specialists and their specialty is not usually transferable across disciplinary boundaries. To be placed on the redeployment list was basically to be consigned to Limbo in the near-certain knowledge that entry into Hell was just a matter of time.

Alternatively, staff could apply for a voluntary redundancy package. This consisted of a payout calculated according to a formula that reflected length of service, rank, and so on. Those who applied for redeployment but could not be redeployed would be awarded voluntary redundancies compulsorily. In effect, they would be jettisoned from the University like household waste onto a skip – although they would be sent a letter purporting to value their service.

Murdo and his senior management were aware, of course, that this would be a 'challenging' time for people, and they did their best to help the staff through their difficulties with two significant measures signalling empathy and concern. First, staff were advised that everyone would be entitled to two free sessions in the 'Employee Assistance Program', which was a counselling scheme run by the Health

Service. The counsellors had probably themselves been through the restructuring of the admin staff and were therefore well qualified to empathise with the new round of victims.

Second, the University intended to learn from certain aspects of the admin restructure that had not gone so well – unlike most of the restructure which had, of course, gone swimmingly. Many of the admin staff had complained that their ordeal was unduly protracted. They had been declared to be affected, then left in a condition of uncertainly for weeks while the University dithered over what to do with them. After that (once the colleges had been created), they were tortured with interviews for the new jobs. Some unfortunates went through this purgatory many times until it was clear that there was no job for them, at which point they were finally made redundant. This had been the fate, for example, of Karen, the manager of the old School of Social Studies.

Murdo and his pals were determined that this kind of cruelty must be avoided when it came to the academic staff. Consequently, when the first of the change proposals were announced in September, it was also declared that everything would be settled by Christmas. That way there would be certainty. Those who had lost their jobs would be able to enjoy a festive season with their families secure in the knowledge that they had nothing whatever to hope for.

***

> Country such Australia is representative democracy, this mean in system of political every citizen vote candidate who represent them, in order carry out and leading commercial on their behalf. However, practice as well as institutions of government's system of Australia reflect north American and british in way is unique Australia.

Since this was an international student, and Medway could more or less understand what the student meant to say, he'd allow the essay a passing grade. This is what he'd come to, he reflected: a gatekeeper for gibberish, although letting it in rather than keeping it out.

It was late and time to pack up. Medway gathered up the books and papers he might need at home, squeezed them into his backpack, and headed off. In the corridor he once again saw something he wished he hadn't. Murdo's face, set in a permanent scowl like a tribal mask, was prominent on a poster that was on display all over the University. The theme of the poster was zero tolerance for bullying. Medway would pass one of these hideous and hypocritical communications every evening on his way out of Hayek South.

Like the Levite in the gospels, he had previously tried to pass by on the other side, although in this case to avoid doing evil rather than good. He succeeded in restraining himself for some weeks. Tonight, however, he finally took out his pen and drew a small but curly moustache under Murdo's nose. On subsequent visits he progressively added a number of other enhancements: crossed eyes, glasses, an eye patch, dark glasses, a pipe, spots of acne, a goatee, Mohican haircut, diabolical horns, protruding antennae. After two weeks, Murdo's face was almost wholly obliterated and the poster was removed.

Medway knew his act of rebellion was pathetic, but in truth few other forms of resistance were possible.

To begin with, the staff tried to use Leichardt's own institutions, starting with the University Council, where this story began. As well as Goldfinger and Murdo, there were several Council members, representing various community 'stakeholders.' Unfortunately, Medway and his colleagues were unlikely to get much relief from this quarter, since most of the Council were toadies and yes-people appointed by Goldfinger. Moreover, the Chancellor and his Council had appointed Murdo, so he was doing what they had hired him to do. Like Henry VIII importing a special French executioner to dispatch Anne Boleyn, the Council had chosen Murdo to decimate the staff. That was what he was doing, faithful to the trust reposed in him. The only difference was that Anne's executioner was a skilled swordsman who could decapitate with a single, deft stroke, while Murdo was more like a thug whose method was to rain blows on the victim with a club – or, more likely, a Gray Nicholls Predator.

Of course, the staff had representatives on the Council. In the past, there had been two members elected by the staff plus two student reps and someone from the union. But Goldfinger had seen to it that these five seats had been reduced to two. The two tried hard to promote the staff's view, but they had little chance against the massed ranks of brown-noses confronting them.

In addition to the Council, there was the Academic Caucus. This had more non-toady potential, since the chairperson and two members were elected by the staff. Whelper, it may be recalled, had been an elected staff representative on the Caucus – although that was scarcely a strong example of independent critical thought. At any rate, the current chair and representatives were all stout defenders of the interests of the staff and students. The problem here was that the Caucus had no decision-making power; it was advisory only.

In short, Leichardt's institutions offered little prospect for holding Murdo to account. In this connection, some people had further observations to make about his enormous salary. Part of the official rationale for this was an analogy with business – Murdo's millions were in line with those raked in by CEOs of commercial enterprises. But attention was drawn to a crucial difference between the two cases. Commercial CEOs were held accountable by their shareholders, who, at least in theory, could object to executive salaries if there was no commensurate performance. In the case of Leichardt's Vice-Chancellor, there was no comparable accountability. The counterparts to shareholders in the University were its 'members', the staff, but they had no control over what the Vice-Chancellor did. He was answerable to the Council and no one else. And again, they would back him because they had appointed him.

Medway tried to picture what things would be like if Leichardt were more democratic. Actually, it wasn't that hard. When he'd first arrived, Heads of Faculty (as they were known then) were elected by the staff of the relevant Faculty. Medway could remember voting for them. If that happened now, what would be the chances of getting someone like Ethel? It was still possible because the demos can make mistakes. But even if an Ethel were elected once, her re-election would be unlikely. Crawlers like Whelper and Sediment would vote for her, no one else.

And imagine if the Vice-Chancellor were elected by the staff of the university. This had never been the practice at Leichardt but it wasn't impossible – there were examples of universities where the leader was elected. If that happened, how likely would it be that they would get someone like Murdo? Again, it was possible but if such an appalling mistake was made it would be correctable at the next election.

Alas, as Medway had so often had occasion to observe in recent years, Leichardt was no democracy. What was it exactly? He wondered how it would be categorised by the sage of Stagira, now languishing at the top of the CHQ amphitheatre, with the recent mocking addition of a Make Leichardt Great cap surmounting the philosopher like a crown of thorns. Aristotle divides forms of political rule into three types: rule by the one, the few, and the many. Each of those forms comes in two versions. The 'perfect' forms are those in which rulers act in the interest of the ruled – namely, monarchy, aristocracy and what Aristotle calls 'polity.' The imperfect or corrupt forms are those in which rule is exercised in the interests of the ruler, and they comprise tyranny, oligarchy, and 'democracy' – the last of these is the word Aristotle reserves for rule by the many in their own interest. The best form of rule varies with the cultural circumstances, but the average best is a combination of aristocracy and polity.

Applying Aristotle's categories, Medway was in no doubt that Leichardt belonged in the imperfect or corrupt camp, since the entire institution now existed to service the inflated salaries and egos of Murdo and his executives. Within that category, Medway was tempted to define Leichardt as a tyranny, an instance of rule by one person in his own interest. In this case it would be a unique kind of tyranny called a Murdocracy. But no doubt that was too simple. Behind Murdo was Goldfinger and the Council, and in front of him were lieutenants like Ethel. So, perhaps it would be more accurate to call Leichardt an oligarchy, a system of rule by a few people in their own interests. Whatever it was, it certainly wasn't a system that paid much attention to the welfare and views of people other than the rulers themselves.

Under these conditions, the staff's best hope for defending its interests was the Union. The vast majority of the staff, including Medway, were members of the Union, and its officials did their best to challenge or at least mitigate the worst effects of Murdo's rampage. Indeed, their efforts were positively heroic. But the Union was constrained by the Enterprise Agreement, the document regulating industrial relations in the University. This was authorised by 'Fair Work' legislation that had been created and refined by successive federal governments, usually those of the conservative Coalition and consequently reflecting the Coalition's neoliberal values.

Under the Enterprise Agreement, disputes between the Union and the University had to be arbitrated at the Fair Work Commission, which usually ruled in favour of the University. Early in the academic restructure, the Union did lodge a dispute with Fair Work, and Murdo's program had to be suspended while the dispute was concluded. This action was portrayed by Murdo as tantamount to an assault on the interests of the staff, who he knew were looking forward to having their jobs removed by Christmas. But, although the Union extracted some concessions, the Fair Work commissioner basically upheld the University's case, and Murdo's purge soon got going again.

One last conduit for protest had been instituted by the University itself: the online *Your Say* survey of staff opinion. This had been carried out some time before the academic restructure commenced, so it did not contain any specific response to Murdo's plan in action. Even so, people had plenty to say in the survey about the principles behind the plan, and about senior management more generally. Medway had taken the survey and made some choice observations about Ethel. The survey results were supposed to be anonymous, but he had taken care nonetheless to identify himself on the form as a disabled indigenous woman aged 40-50.

He was not the only staff member with critical points to make. There were signs that the survey contained some results that were embarrassing for the University, the main sign being that the University refused to release it. In the end, Alex Euripides and other staff from Law managed to force its release by using a Freedom of Information process. The figures from the survey were revealed, along with some of the comments people had entered, although the full range of comments was permanently embargoed.

The figures from the survey were, indeed, suboptimal. In the area of 'leadership', the University received a favourable rating from only one-third of its staff, which was 18% lower than the average among Australian and New Zealand universities. The statement, 'I have confidence in the ability of senior management' received the agreement of only 28% of the staff. Ethel's results for her leadership of the College of Non-Sciences were similar.

Such were the views of the staff. But it is one thing for the staff's feelings to be made known, quite another for that knowledge to have any effect on executives like Murdo. He remained secure in his conviction that he was acting for the best, and his attack on the staff continued.

More informal kinds of resistance began to coalesce around those people who were prepared to stick their heads above the parapet. Medway admired and supported them, but he was not one of them. Still punch-drunk after being one of Ethel's human targets while he was a dean, he was keeping a low profile. Apart from his contribution to the *Your Say* survey, he did little except listen to what was going on, read his emails, talk to people behind closed doors, and deface Murdo's anti-bullying poster.

More courageous people attempted to resist in more constructive ways, and those best placed to do so were the Leichardt Distinguished Professors. Possessing a status something like that of 'made men' in the Mafia, they were untouchable because the University had publicly declared them to be its finest. While most of the staff were wary of speaking out too loudly against Murdo's agenda, the Distinguished Professors could get away with it because the University needed their research publications, grants and reputation. Of course, not all of them exploited this advantage, the scientists on the whole saying little. But some Leichardt Distinguished Professors became leaders of the emerging insurgency.

The most high-profile of these leaders was Professor Cardigan, the Leichardt Distinguished Professor of public health policy. Incensed by Murdo's agenda, she applied herself to opposing it, becoming the de facto host of an email discussion group in which the latest atrocities and injustices were reported and suggestions made about how to respond.

Cardigan also worked at producing a public statement that would capture some of the widely shared objections to what was going on. Together with two other Leichardt Distinguished Professors, she went to see Murdo in person to try to intercede with him. Predictably, he was unmoved by their arguments, but they left with one concession. They did get permission to address a special meeting of the Council that was scheduled for December. The staff were permitted to be present at the address too. It promised to be a rare opportunity to bear collective witness to a historic moment.

16

ACADEMIC INTEGRITY

It was late on Friday afternoon and Medway was looking forward to going home, but he had another academic integrity case to deal with. According to the papers he'd been sent, a Business undergraduate called Phil Smith was accused of copying an entire essay from unacknowledged internet sources. So far, so routine. 'Phil Smith' sounded familiar, though. Where had Medway heard that name before?

There was a knock on the door and the student entered. He was mature, in his mid-thirties, tall, athletic and gingery. His face had a rich orange hue, like that of a healthy version of Donald Trump, suggesting country origins or outdoor work. It was Sarah's tree surgeon.

'Phil! Good heavens, I thought I recognised your name. Come in.'

'Hello, Prof,' said Phil.

'But aren't you a tree surgeon?'

'I am,' said Phil, 'but I want to move on. I'm at uni studying business part-time so I can become a financial adviser.'

Medway gestured him to a chair at the round, plastic meeting table and joined him there.

'I have to say, this doesn't look good,' said Medway. 'According to the information your lecturer has given me, you've simply copied the whole of your essay from internet sources without acknowledgement. Do you accept that's what you've done?'

'Yes.' The orange face looked impassive.

'Do you understand this is plagiarism, which is a serious violation of the University's rules of academic integrity?'

'Yes.' Phil looked serious and respectful but not obviously concerned.

'Okay. One thing I have to do in cases like this is check the University's "confidential register" to see if you've done this before. I've checked and found that it's the third time you've done this. Do you know what that means?'

'No.' Medway suspected that Phil did know.

'It's now a serious matter. The first time we give you the benefit of the doubt and assume you didn't do it deliberately. The second time it's obviously deliberate and you get a sharper warning. If you still do the same thing after that, it looks as though you're not taking the matter seriously and have no intention of complying with the rules. Cases like that I refer to the College's academic integrity officer, who usually sends it on to the Deputy Vice-Chancellor (Students) with a recommendation for disciplinary action at University level.

Various penalties are possible, including permanent exclusion from the University.' Medway briefly wondered whether that was really a penalty, but it was all he'd got. At this point students usually became agitated and often turned into blubbering wrecks. Phil stoically offered no comment.

'You don't seem bothered,' said Medway. 'Do you have anything to say in mitigation?'

'What's "mitigation"?'

'Something that improves the situation or makes it less bad. Like climate change mitigation.'

'What's "climate change"?'

'Never mind. I mean, can you give me any explanation or any background information that might give me a reason to treat you more leniently?'

Phil still stared at him vacantly.

'Do you have any excuses?' said Medway.

'This degree is really important to me,' Phil said.

'That's good to hear but it doesn't help me much,' said Medway. 'Most students' degrees are important to them but they don't plagiarise their work.' He wasn't sure whether either of these claims was true, but they sounded like the kind of thing he should say.

Phil sat there. He seemed to be on the verge of saying something but still said nothing.

'Right, well if there's nothing you can add I'll have to send the papers to the College academic integrity officer and she'll take it from there.'

'Wait,' said Phil, suddenly urgent. 'Could I make a deal?'

'What do you mean?'

'Look, do you know who I am?'

'Sorry, I don't follow.' Was Phil really Brad Pitt in disguise?

'I'm Byron Scape. I used to play test cricket for Australia.'

'Good God! I thought I recognised you from somewhere.' Yes, by imagining Phil in a batting helmet, he could see it was true. In which case … 'So, why are you calling yourself Phil Smith?'

'I'm trying to rebuild my life after what happened in the West Indies. I need a new start.'

'But I thought you were making pots of money playing for the Chennai Checkbooks.'

'Didn't last,' said Scape sadly. 'I got caught up in a match-fixing problem and they let me go.'

'Really. I didn't hear anything about that.'

'They hushed it up. That was the end of my cricket career. I've been trying to get a start in business. The thing is, I need this qualification.'

'All right, I can see how that might be. But I'm still not sure how I can help. This is your third academic integrity offence and I have to apply the rules.'

'Here's the thing,' said Phil. 'I know Murdo is giving you guys a hard time.'

'Ye-es …'

'I know what that's like,' said Phil. 'Come Christmas, half of you will be gone.'

'Maybe …'

'Well, maybe I could help you.'

'How would you do that?' This was getting positively sulphurous.

'I've got some stuff on Murdo. Evidence that he ordered me to tamper with the ball and then paid me off to keep me quiet.'

'My God, what kind of evidence?'

Scape had clearly come prepared for this, at least as a last resort. Out of his bag he pulled an ancient cassette recorder containing a tape. Pressing 'play', he treated Medway to a piece of secret history. Although the sound quality was poor, through a curtain of hums and crackles the voices of Murdo and Scape were recognisable. In a discourse laced with casual obscenities, Murdo said just what Scape claimed, ending with the comment,

'Thanks, mate, I'm glad we're on the same page. We'll both be better off this way and no cunt will be the wiser.'

Medway was speechless.

'So, you see how I can help you, Prof. You make my little problem go away and I'll give you a copy of my tape.'

'Why haven't you used this before now?'

'It's my insurance; I was waiting for the right moment.'

Medway had just enough presence of mind to realise that he ought to put an end to this conversation immediately and send Scape packing, but the thought of Murdo on the rack of public opinion was too delicious. And, of course, beyond that lay further attractive prospects. Even Leichardt would find it hard to retain as Vice-Chancellor someone who had been exposed as a liar and fraud on such a scale. It would be the end of Murdo, and, with his departure, the discrediting of everything and everyone to do with him, including Target 1% and Goldfinger.

It was just too tempting.

'I'll have to think about this,' said Medway, trying to sound like a professional academic rather than an underworld conspirator. 'I'll get back to you next week.'

'Thanks, Prof, you know where to find me,' said Scape.

***

'Do it, Geoffrey. You don't owe those people anything,' said Sarah that evening. 'I'd love to see Murdo exposed publicly. It's just what he deserves.'

Sarah had robust moral convictions, driven by emotion and untroubled by second thoughts or fine distinctions. When it came to the question of what to do with the culpable, she was given to recommending castration followed by 'stringing up by the goolies.' While the logician in Medway could see the practical difficulty with this, he could also appreciate Sarah's muscular sense of justice. Murdo certainly deserved something extremely unpleasant.

Still, Medway was not a political philosopher for nothing, and he was able to complicate the issue without too much difficulty. Over what seemed like an interminable weekend, he oscillated among a series of considerations in an anguish of indecision.

At breakfast on Saturday morning he began by ruminating on a straightforward Benthamite act-utilitarian position, which seemed to support Sarah's view. 'The greatest good of the greatest number' – that was Bentham's formula, understanding by 'good' what made people happy, which in turn meant what gave them pleasure. Skewering Murdo would probably please a lot more people than it would upset. The 'affected' staff of Leichardt would be delighted for a start, not to mention the scores of people Murdo had harmed over the years in sport, business and personal relations. More importantly, exposing Murdo would surely discredit his program. If the restructure was halted, that would definitely increase human happiness. So, act utilitarians would say, yes, do it.

But then, sitting in his hut afterwards, Medway began to think about more sophisticated utilitarians, like Mill, the subject of his D. Phil. thesis and first book all those years ago. Mill would agree with Bentham that we should maximise human happiness but add that the way to do this is to focus not on individual acts but on general rules. The question is, what are the rules that usually increase human happiness? One of the standard contenders is the rule against lying. Without that, social relations will break down because people won't trust one another. Medway would certainly have to lie if he went along with Scape's deal. So, on this score, Mill would probably say, no, don't do it.

On the other hand, there was another side to Mill, according to which we shouldn't just follow conventional rules without thinking for ourselves about their nature and effect. Lying may usually be wrong, but it would be right to lie if that was necessary to save someone from the Nazis, for example. Might there be a good reason for lying in the Scape versus Murdo case? Perhaps so, if it led to the best consequences. Didn't that just lead back to the rules? Well, you had to remember, too, that for Mill the best consequences were not just about any old idea of human happiness, but about human happiness conceived in terms of the 'higher' pleasures, those involved in the more elevated aspects of human experience – for example, the pleasures of exercising one's own critical judgement. In that case, one might reflect that pleasures of that kind were under threat from Murdo, whose program reduced everything to what was necessary to make money. So, this aspect of Mill might support making the deal with Scape.

Then again, there were uncertainties. By lunchtime it occurred to Medway that any kind of utilitarianism required a calculation of consequences, and since these stretched into the future they were sometimes – often in fact – less than obvious. What if Medway's collusion with Phil got out? Also, might there not be some way of achieving the greatest good, the defeat of Murdo, without Medway's violating his obligations to the university? Maybe utilitarianism just didn't give any clear answer at all.

Mention of obligations suggested a Kantian approach and also reminded Medway that he had to mow the lawn. After lunch, while he was mowing, he recalled Kant's categorical imperative and its demand that we follow rules that can be accepted by all reasonable persons. As in the case of Mill, one of the classic Kantian examples was the rule against lying. So, Kant would probably say, no, don't do it.

Or would he? On Saturday evening, recumbent in front of a television rerun of *Foyle's War*, Medway began to wonder whether Kantian thinking condemns lying quite so dogmatically. Kant advanced several different formulations of the categorical imperative, including one known as 'the duty to respect persons.' This said that one should always treat people as autonomous beings, never as mere instruments. Now, lying was traditionally held up as an instance of treating people as instruments, so on this score respect for persons seemed to go against the pro-Scape view. On the other hand, what was Murdo doing if not treating people as instruments? Moreover, he was doing that on a massive scale compared with the little fib – a white lie, really? – that Medway was contemplating. In that case, maybe Kant would actually approve of Phil's deal.

The following morning, in the shower – so often a place of inspiration for Medway – he wondered what Aristotle would say. Well, he would say, live in accordance with 'the virtues.' But what were they? One was courage, and accepting Phil's deal would certainly be courageous because of the risks involved. But another was 'practical wisdom', or knowing, through experience, the right thing to do in the situation. But what the hell was that?

One way of finding out is to imitate known, experienced, practically wise persons. Who did Medway know who fell into this category? Did Sarah possess practical wisdom? If so, he knew what she'd say. What about Beadle? He was an experienced person who would say the exact opposite to Sarah. Beadle didn't care for Murdo either, but Medway was sure that Beadle, the ex-head prefect, would urge him to do his institutional duty and nail Scape to the wall; the Murdo matter would have to be dealt with in some other way. Aristotle's virtue ethics had something to it – you had to look at the situation, not just the rule – but there was a frustrating indeterminacy about it. The answer you got depended on which experienced person you decided to imitate, and you could more or less guarantee the answer by choosing the person to give it. This was a point well made by Sartre, who was otherwise a major French idiot on a level with Foucault.

On Sunday afternoon, waiting in a checkout line in a supermarket, Medway came to the subject of Nietzsche. What would the *enfant terrible* of Sils Maria have to say? Rather than struggle with that, Medway decided to go with the advice of P. G. Wodehouse, expressed through the sage medium of Jeeves: 'Nietzsche is not sound.' One genuine contribution made by Foucault to ethics was to serve as a warning of what can happen if you take Nietzsche too seriously.

Finally, in the dead watches of Sunday night, when he couldn't sleep, Medway arrived at the 'value pluralism' sketched by people like Isaiah Berlin and Max Weber. The pluralists say that the most fundamental human values are multiple, conflicting and incommensurable. So, for example, when liberty and equality conflict, there's no reason to say that liberty is always more important than equality, or equality more important than liberty. The best you can do is make a judgement that addresses the particular circumstances. Now, this may not seem much of a help, but Medway found that the pluralist view at least clarified what was fundamentally at stake in his dilemma. Basically, it all boiled down to a choice between stopping Murdo and punishing Scape. Which was more important here and now?

In those terms it was a no-brainer: stopping Murdo was more important than punishing Scape. There were risks involved, but he'd have to be brave. So, yes, he'd do it!

***

On Monday morning he was back in the office and ready to phone Scape with the good news.

Who was he kidding? He couldn't do it. He would love to accept Scape's extraordinary deal, but it just wasn't possible for him. If he did, he would be entering the world of Scape and Murdo, and he'd never get back. He would be one of them. He would probably be found out eventually and exposed as a liar and cheat, just like the cricketers. There would always be that possibility: if Scape could betray Murdo (although not without reason), he could betray Medway too. But even if Scape didn't betray him, Medway himself would know what he'd done. He'd be a different person, someone he didn't want to be. It was nothing to be smug about; it was a failure in a way. Why couldn't he follow Machiavelli's advice to the prince to learn how not to be virtuous, especially in a world where you're surrounded by the vicious? Well, he wasn't especially virtuous but he didn't want to be vicious either. He was no prince. It wasn't going to happen.

He sent the case up the line to the College academic integrity officer, and phoned Scape to say what he'd done. Scape took it remarkably well. Perhaps he fancied his chances of making a deal with the next integrity officer. At any rate, he gave Medway the strong impression that he knew what he wanted to do next.

17

SCANDAL

Murdo felt a wet kiss on his cheek and surfaced into a groggy consciousness. That had been some night last night – at least that part of it he could remember. Perhaps he shouldn't have insisted on that third bottle of Grange. But these Vice-Chancellor conferences were boring enough, you had to make them bearable somehow.

He looked up at the naked woman who was, it seemed, floating above him like a balloon party-animal fashioned by a pornographer. Courtney looked good first thing in the morning, and you couldn't say that of all women. More to the point, her performance in the sack last night had been nothing short of sensational. This was the true meaning of 'executive assistant'! It was a pity she was married, and a nuisance that *he* was married – although in his case Shannon wouldn't let him in the house, so that wasn't such a problem in practical terms.

'Courtney, who said you could be out of bed? I feel the need for another briefing coming on.'

'Your wish is usually my command, Murdo, but we're running late. We need to be at the airport by 9.30 at the latest. Now, don't pout. I need about 15 minutes in the bathroom, then it will be all yours.'

'Okay, but we need to continue last night's dialogue as soon as possible.'

While Courtney slipped into the bathroom, Murdo reached for the television remote and switched on. The morning programs he liked to watch were those on the commercial channels, which concentrated on jokes and advertisements, even during the so-called 'news.' But these days people expected him to know what was going on, so he felt obliged to watch the proper news on the public broadcaster.

The flat screen pinged into being, and Murdo was treated to the usual procession of grimness – a plane disappearance, the Russians bombing some place, the Chinese torturing people in a 're-education' camp (interesting, must make a note of that), the Americans torturing people in Guantanamo (also interesting: could Leichardt get a campus off-shore?), another ruckus in federal parliament. At least, all this stuff was enlivened by the daily Twitter contributions of the President of the United States. The man was a truly weird individual, no doubt, but he was hated and despised by every single academic Murdo had ever met, and that alone was a major point in his favour. Frankly, Murdo found a lot to like in the great orange giant: a plain speaker, unafraid to reject the advice of supposed 'experts' on climate change (which was a hoax), and someone who was prepared to deal with opponents as they deserved to be dealt with – that is, wiped from the face of the earth. If ever there was a master of mental disintegration, it was the current POTUS.

All too soon, the politically correct apparatchik presenting the news – almost certainly gay – passed on to matters less entertaining. Something about trade figures ... Murdo was losing interest.

But then things picked up. 'In breaking news,' read the pansy. This was more like it, thought Murdo. 'Breaking news' stories were usually more gripping. An invasion, or death of a famous person, or the sudden collapse of the international financial system, that kind of thing.

'We have received a tape recording relating to the ball-tampering scandal in which the Australian test cricket team was embroiled 15 years ago. In the tape, Murdo McMurdo, who was then captain of the test team and who has since become Vice-Chancellor of Leichardt University, can be heard admitting that he had ordered Byron Scape, the young batsman, to tamper with the ball. He can also be heard assuring Scape of a lucrative Indian Premier League contract if Scape took sole responsibility in public for the tampering. The authenticity of the tape has been established independently. This confirms suspicions that have long been held in cricket circles and beyond ...'

Murdo stared at the screen, momentarily dumbfounded.

Recovering somewhat, he screamed, 'That fucking piece of shit, Scape!' at the top of his lungs, making Courtney drop the soap in alarm.

'What is it, Murdo?'

'It's that fucking piece of shit Scape! I'll explain in the limo. We've got to get out of here.'

By the time they got to the airport, the vultures were gathering. The media pack spotted them just as they scampered into the Qantas VIP Lounge, where they would be safe for a while but not for long. The walk from the Lounge to first-class boarding was like an especially violent game of footy, with Murdo as the footy. The same thing happened when they landed and when Murdo got home. The nightmare had begun.

***

The following day, Murdo issued a press statement: 'There is no truth whatever to the story currently being run by the public broadcaster concerning my role in the ball tampering offence committed by Byron Scape in the West Indies fifteen years ago. The story is fake news, and I'm currently obtaining legal advice on the matter.'

But then a steady stream of people began to come forward attesting to Murdo's character and history, and their testimony was not complimentary. His old teammate Tadger said he wasn't surprised by the revelation and asserted that Murdo was a liar and manipulator who had wrecked his cricket career and broken up his marriage. Several former England players described the PTSD they experienced after their mental disintegration brought about by Murdo. Former business associates and employees gave instances of Murdo's indifference to the truth and painted him as, basically, a fraud.

His first ex, Tonya, described him as a sexist bully with a controlling personality, and hinted at incidents of domestic violence. Luckily, nothing had been heard so far from his second ex, Sharon.

What the media itself called the 'media pile-on' was so vigorous that public opinion began to shift. Polls that had originally shown a good deal of support for Murdo, based largely on his status as a cricket legend, now began to turn sharply against him. The view became widespread that the former sporting hero was, in fact, a first-class – indeed, international-standard – shit.

Murdo decided to change tack. Abandoning his attempt simply to deny what he'd done, he would shift to a position more likely to attract public sympathy. He hit on the notion of disability, which seemed to be like a religion these days. Some sob story about how he had not been responsible for his actions would be hard to argue with. Stories like this worked for everyone else, why not for him too?

To get the story out there, he needed an intimate, revelatory interview with a friendly journalist on national television. He floated the idea with his old pals at Channel Nine and asked for the famous cricket commentator, Jim Dixon. Jim would bowl him some gentle pies and not question his fabrications. Indeed, Jim's famous voice would add credibility to Murdo's tale. Channel Nine agreed, and Dixon was only too delighted to help out poor old Murdo, the innocent victim of a savage campaign of envy and vilification.

On the morning of the interview, Murdo arrived at Channel Nine looking forward to vindication. He was shown to the green room, where he relaxed with an early snifter. A lackey with an identification lanyard approached, no doubt to say how wonderful it was to have Murdo come in.

'Good morning, Professor McMurdo,' said the lackey. *Professor* – he still got a charge out of that! 'I'm sorry but Jim Dixon has been taken ill and is unavailable for the interview. He sends his apologies. However, Sharon Prenupple is available and happy to take over.'

'What?!' shrieked Murdo, his eyes goggling. He could feel the blood draining from his face. Sharon was his second ex, and their parting had not been friendly.

'I'm sorry but that's all we can offer at this point in time.'

Murdo weighed up his options. If he allowed Sharon to interview him, it could be a disaster. She was just the kind of vindictive bitch who would take advantage of his temporary weakness. On the other hand, if he refused the interview, that news would itself get out and he would be made to look even more guilty in the eyes of the public. On balance, he decided, he'd be better off risking it. He could handle Sharon; he always had the past.

'Sure,' he said, trying to sound cheerfully indifferent, 'Sharon will be fine.'

They ushered him into the recording studio, where Sharon came forward to peck him on the cheek.

'Murdo, Darling! So good to see you. It's been too long.'

'Hi, Sharon, yes it has,' said Murdo. 'You're looking gorgeous, mate!' She was, too. Tall, slim, blonde and blue-eyed. Why had they split up? He couldn't remember; it now seemed a poor decision.

'Thank you, Murdo, so are you. And so intellectually distinguished these days too!' Was there a hint of sarcasm there? If so, it was well disguised.

'Now, I hope you're not going to be too tough on me. I've been through a lot over the past few days, and I just want to tell my side of the story.'

'Yes, of course. Don't worry. I have Jim Dixon's questions here, and all they do is give you an opportunity to tell your story.'

Murdo felt a wave of relief. Sharon really did seem genuinely happy to see him; not aggressive at all. Everything was going to be all right.

'Now, if you'd just have a seat here, we'll get makeup over and touch you up.'

'Always happy to be touched up,' said Murdo, making the most of his famous larrikin wit to lighten the atmosphere, although he wasn't sure about the look Sharon gave him when he said that.

Twenty minutes later, the preparations were complete, theme music sounded and the cameras focused on Sharon's intro.

'For tonight's special interview, we welcome Professor Murdo McMurdo, Vice-Chancellor of Leichardt University and former Australian test cricket captain. Welcome Professor McMurdo.'

'Please, Sharon, call me Murdo.'

'Thank you, Murdo. Now, allegations have resurfaced that you ordered Byron Scape to tamper with the ball in the Third Test against the West Indies some fifteen years ago, and also that you essentially paid Scape for his silence afterwards. Are these allegations true?'

This was a bit more abrupt than Murdo had imagined, but it was the fundamental question and he was prepared for it.

'Well, yes, but I need to explain the circumstances.'

'So, you admit to cheating in the test match, then covering up your part in it afterwards.' Sharon's tone was distinctly cold and accusatory. Murdo was beginning to remember why they'd split up.

'Please let me explain what was going on. Yes, I did those things, and I'm sorry if anyone was offended by them. But I was suffering at the time from post-traumatic stress disorder.'

'Really, what was the trauma?'

'My doctor diagnosed something with a very long name I can't now remember, but I think of it as "loseritis."'

'Loseritis?'

'Yes. We'd just lost the first two tests of the series and we were all suffering from the trauma of those defeats. The baggy green had been trampled into the dust and we were all hurting. The dressing room was very quiet. Tadger was right off his grub.'

'Go on.'

'Well, at that low point I was suffering from a compulsive desire to make up for our failures by winning at all costs. I see now it was wrong but at the time I couldn't help myself.'

'So, ordering Scape to tamper with the ball was not a deliberate act you were responsible for but a compulsion. It was out of your control.' That was indeed Murdo's message but this time the tinge of sarcasm in Sharon's voice was unmistakable.

'Well, yes it was.' The studio lights seemed to be getting hotter.

'And then, throwing Byron Scape to the wolves afterwards, when he had just done what you told him – that was also something you had no control over.' The sarcastic tinge had taken on the colour of Murdo's blood.

'Sharon, you don't know the pressure we were under. Those defeats had been devastating. It was what it must be like for soldiers in a war they're losing. They see their friends destroyed, they don't know whether they might be next. That's what it was like for us.'

'So, now you're comparing yourself to our war veterans? People who've been killed, injured and traumatised in armed conflicts overseas. Losing a test cricket match is like that?'

'Well, it's not exactly the same, of course, but it was still traumatising. That's all I'm saying.' Murdo was beginning to panic, his eyes bulging.

'Right. So, let me be clear about all this,' said Sharon. 'You're saying you cheated in a test match and then covered it up, sacrificing the career of a young cricketer in the process – someone new to the team, who you were responsible for leading and mentoring, who was overawed and intimidated by you. But you're not really responsible for any of that because you'd lost the previous two matches.'

'Sharon, you make it sound sub-optimal, but you're not seeing it from my point of view.'

'Murdo, isn't the truth pretty simple here? You're a liar, a coward and a fraud. You're someone who should never have been leading a national sports team and who should not be occupying any kind of leadership role now.'

Before the interview, Murdo had thought about simulating a bit of weeping at a strategic stage of the conversation, perhaps at the point where he revealed the deep trauma that had forced him to perform those regrettable actions. He'd put the idea aside because he didn't think he was a good enough actor to carry off the necessary simulation. But now, genuinely traumatised, he found he had no problem weeping quite sincerely.

Once they were off-air, Murdo sat in a catatonic state for some minutes while people were on the move around him.

'Murdo, are you still with us?' asked Sharon, bending over him to check whether he was breathing.

'But Sharon,' he managed to whisper, 'you said that all you were going to do was ask me the questions Jim had prepared.'

'No, Murdo,' Sharon said. 'I said I *had* Jim's list of questions. I didn't say I was going to use them.'

***

The interview went to air that evening, and Murdo immediately received a call from Goldfinger to come and see him in his office downtown first thing in the morning. That's it, thought Murdo, I'm finished.

Arriving at the law chambers of Hunt, Flay and Goldfinger, Murdo was kept waiting for 30 minutes before he was admitted to the squat presence of the Chancellor.

'I'll be honest, Murdo,' said Goldfinger, 'it would have been better if you hadn't given that interview.'

'I see that now, Goldy. It was an ambush.'

'If you wander into the middle of the jungle, that's what happens.'

'Okay, so I assume you want my resignation.'

Goldfinger looked genuinely surprised. 'What gave you that idea?'

'Well, the scandal, the harm to the reputation of Leichardt.'

'Oh, I wouldn't worry about that.'

'No?'

'My dear Murdo, no public figure resigns because of reputation-harming scandals these days.'

'They don't?'

'Just look at the recent record. The President of the United States is quite obviously a compulsive liar, womaniser and thug, not to mention a menace to Western democracy. Has he resigned?'

'Not yet.'

'No, and he never will. Your namesake Rupert presided over the worst scandal there's ever been in UK journalism but did he resign?'

'No.'

'And if you want examples closer to home, just look at the federal government. Almost the entire front bench are knaves or incompetents. Think of the minister known as 'Dracula', who spent years pursuing welfare recipients for money they didn't owe. Or the bloke whose "office" sent that fraudulent email about the Mayor of Sydney. Or that dufus who went off to the cricket (no offence) in the middle of a crisis in his department. Or the Deputy PM, with his in-house affair and general buffoonery. For Christ's sake, the PM himself is a walking disaster, what with the lying, bullying, pork-barrelling, backgrounding, gaslighting, sexism, and refusal to take responsibility for anything. I could go on. Everyone knows all about this stuff. How many of these people have resigned?'

'Would it be none?'

'Correct. It's just not done. Sure, you've been exposed in the national media as a cheat, a liar, a bully, a sexist pig, a manipulator ...'

'Gee, don't hold back, Goldy.'

'... an abysmal leader, a ruthless, self-serving piece of shit. My point is, so what? These things are irrelevant. No, I take that back. They are exactly the qualities you need to do what the Council and I want you to do. What matters is that you're doing a great job at Leichardt, just as we asked. We'll back you.'

Murdo began to feel hot tears welling up again, this time out of gratitude. 'Thanks, Goldy, I appreciate it. But what if they come after you?'

'What are they going to do? The Council and I are not really accountable to anyone. Yes, in theory Leichardt is governed by an Act of Parliament, but in practice the state and federal governments leave us alone to do what we want.

As far as they're concerned, the universities are independent bodies that govern themselves. That's the government's excuse for not funding us properly, so the payoff for us is that we're effectively autonomous. They don't support us, so we can do as we like. Which means, in reality, the Council can do as it likes. Which in turn means, if you want the brutal reality, Murdo, …'

'I do, Goldy.'

'… I thought so. The reality is, *I* can do as *I* like.'

'That's reassuring, mate.'

'It should be. So, Murdo, put all this bullshit out of your mind. Sure, they'll be yelping about it for the next few days, maybe a couple of weeks. But then they'll be distracted by something else and it will blow over. What's the old Arab proverb? "The dogs bark and the caravan moves on."'

Goldfinger was right. Murdo's revolting personality and history remained in the public spotlight for another ten days but was then superseded by yet another scandal in the federal parliament. Whatever Murdo's critics might say, he – and consequently his program – would survive at Leichardt.

18

ETHEL STRIKES

The staff of the College of Non-Sciences received an email from Ethel. This is it, thought Medway, the hour is at hand and the firing squad is assembling. But it was just a foreshadowing. The message noted the commencement of Murdo's academic restructure and announced that Ethel's College would start its consultation process 'in the middle of October.' The message also said, 'I wish to reassure you that there will be <u>no decrease</u> in continuing staff positions across the College.' This did seem somewhat reassuring at the time. It was only in retrospect that Medway looked more closely at Ethel's wording and saw that it made no commitment to any particular distribution of the positions or to maintaining any particular position.

Weeks passed as, one by one, the other colleges published their change proposals. In the natural sciences it wasn't so bad, but even there some units lost one or two people. At the personal level, the process left in its wake a range of stories: of happy immunities (the 'out of scope' and 'unaffected'), of close escapes (those 'affected' but restored to their posts or transferred to teaching-specialist positions, and the rare cases of the redeployed), and of personal disaster (the affected and disposable). Two months later the process was well advanced everywhere else but had still not commenced in the College of Non-Sciences. So much for the consultation beginning in mid-October.

Then at last, in late November, with only a month to go before the end of the University year and Murdo's humanitarian deadline, Ethel sent out another email announcing her intentions. First, there would be a 'staff forum' where the changes would be discussed; then the proposed changes were to be announced immediately *after* the forum.

Many people expressed puzzlement. Why was the College's process so slow to get going? And how was the forum going to work, since it invited the staff to discuss changes that they wouldn't know about until afterwards? Cynics suggested that this curious way of ordering things was a deliberate means of muting any criticism before it arose, and of leaving as little time as possible for objections.

Experts in 'the politics of Ethel', as it had come to be known, were unsurprised by such an ingenious policy. Medway was reminded of the episode in *Catch-22* when Major Major announces that people will be allowed into his office to speak to him only when he is not in his office to hear what they have to say. Similarly, Ethel would be available at the forum when the staff did not know what was in the change proposal, but once the proposal was out she would be back in the Bunker. It wasn't that she was afraid of the staff – on the contrary, most of them were beneath her contempt – rather, the policy was designed to cause maximum confusion and frustration.

On the day of the forum, expectation, speculation, and anticipation ran at fever pitch. The meeting was held in one of the larger teaching rooms where Medway had often addressed the keen, uncomprehending faces of the international students. Soon, Ethel would be doing the same with the staff. The room was rapidly full to overflowing, packed with companies of Business lecturers, caseloads of lawyers, and parties of political scientists. Plume was off sick, as usual, and Euripides was away at a conference, but Millicent, Pleonexia, Whelper, Nick and Professor Cardigan were all there. Medway studied his tense, expectant colleagues. Beads of sweat formed on foreheads, faces were marked by the furtive, hyper-alert expressions of hunted animals.

Ethel entered with her entourage: Sediment and various other cup-bearers, arse-wipers and hangers-on. Ethel herself was in good form. She joked bleakly with her retainers and acknowledged some of her current favourites in the audience, including Pleonexia and Whelper. Then she called the meeting to order and they were underway.

Ethel was a seasoned public performer and on this special occasion she did not disappoint. An act worthy of Meryl Streep was not only delivered but inhabited and gloried in. The basic theme was that Murdo's agenda was on its way, that the staff had had plenty of warning of the sort of changes that it was going to bring, and that there was nothing they could do about it. Those who disagreed with it or did not like it were persons whose aspirations no longer aligned with those of the University. Here and there, Ethel would throw in some hollow acknowledgement of the upheaval all this would cause in some lives, along with pro forma expressions of concern. Mention was made of Murdo's desire to get the nastiness over as quickly as possible for everyone's sake, and of the Employee Assistance Program. But the basic message was that they had got away with their failures, backsliding and indolence for too long and a just nemesis had finally caught up with them. Basically, they had to eat their livers.

Her harangue complete, Ethel smiled menacingly and called for questions. This was less an invitation than a dare. Give it your best shot, you pathetic pieces of shit. Whatever you can throw at me, I'm more than equal to it. Go ahead, punks, make my day!

Like a moth to Ethel's flame, Pleonexia fluttered into life, asking a harmless Dorothy Dixer about the next steps in Ethel's decision-making timeline.

'Thank you, Pleonexia,' said Ethel, 'and let me say what excellent leadership you've shown in the Government discipline, especially over workload issues. Many people are now meeting their targets who were not doing that when you took over, and that's because of your hard work.' Vintage Ethel: divide and rule. Whatever critical edge someone might have read into Pleonexia's ingratiating question was neutralised by the oily stream of Ethel's flattery. The truth was that before Pleonexia took over only one Government person was not meeting his workload target, and he was a recent arrival. Moreover, Pleonexia had had little to do with workload issues. She had been bewildered by the intricacy of the workload plan, and in the end begged Medway to do it for her.

Whelper, witnessing Ethel's buttering up of Pleonexia, saw an opportunity to apply some unction of his own. 'Ethel, I think it's only fair to acknowledge your own excellent leadership at this difficult time,' he honked.

'Thank you, Bruno, that's much appreciated,' said Ethel, smoothly. 'Your contribution should be recognised too.'

For a moment, looks of incomprehension vied with expressions of nausea as people struggled to conceive of what exactly Whelper's 'contribution' had been. But the spell was broken by Professor Cardigan, who introduced a different tone.

'Ethel, this festival of mutual admiration is delightful but I have a couple of questions. First, it's a mystery to me, as it is to many people, why your proposal has taken so long to be released compared with those of other colleges. Can you explain that, please? Second, why are we having this meeting before rather than after the release of the proposal?

'Thank you, Kate. I'm sorry but there had been many calls on my attention over the previous two months, and the issues had been concerning the restructure have been complex. As for the timing of the meeting before the release of the proposal, I want to prepare the staff with some general comments before you see the document. That way, we'll avoid potential misunderstandings and unnecessary upset.

The arrangement had been made entirely with your benefit in mind.'

Cardigan was plainly unimpressed and was about to pursue Ethel when Nick put his hand up.

'May I ask a question?' he inquired with his customary politeness and belief in fundamental human goodness.

'By all means.'

'Many people are worried about the effects on this restructure of the research expectations that have recently been brought out. The demands for external grant money are especially concerning. In effect, these demands are being applied retrospectively. We're being judged right now for our grant-income performance over the past three years, but during that period we were given no warning that this would happen. These demands have come out of the blue. Are you able to reassure us that we will at least be given some time to adjust to these new expectations?'

Ethel squinted menacingly at Nick from the corner of her eye. The squint contained a mixture of irritation and dismissal.

'There's been plenty of warning that this is the University's direction for years now. The current Vice-Chancellor is merely continuing a policy begun by his predecessor eight years ago.'

'Well,' said Cardigan, returning to the fray, 'it's true that there's been talk for some time about the desirability of external grants. But it's never been made clear that getting grants is a condition for keeping our jobs. Again, if that's true, this has just been dropped on us out of nowhere, as Nick says.'

'External grants have been emphasised for years,' Ethel replied impatiently, as if explaining simple arithmetic to a moron, 'and you've had plenty of time to adjust to that priority.'

The back-and-forth continued. People would line up to make critical points or beg desperately for information; Ethel would either gleefully shoot them down or co-opt the questioner as it took her fancy. The basic problem was, as Ethel well knew, that without the change proposal in front of them, the staff were stumbling about in the dark, lashing out at shadows.

'Come on, let's have some more questions,' Ethel taunted, now nicely warmed up. But the gathering had fallen silent, exasperated or cowed into submission. Cardigan and Nick were shaking their heads with frustration. Even Millicent, after an outburst of shouting, was a spent force. Medway found himself once again toying with the idea of Ethelicide. What if he simply rushed up and stabbed her in the carotid artery with his ball-point pen? Again there were drawbacks: a lot of witnesses, for one; Ethel's lack of a neck, for another.

Meanwhile, Ethel had begun to lose interest. Tired of tormenting such a pitiful crowd of zeros, she called a halt. They were ordered to disperse to their rooms and expect the proposal document to be emailed later that afternoon. They filed back to their cells to await their fate.

***

The change proposal came through so late that there was no time to get inquiries answered before the close of business. The document covered the proposed changes to posts throughout the College. Each unit was given its own section, which consisted of a general spiel about what its strengths and priorities were supposed to be, followed by a table setting out the existing posts, with no names attached, comparing these with what was being proposed.

In the case of Medway's Government section, the general spiel said that its strengths were in public administration and international relations. There was no mention of political theory. So much for Medway's self-image, and the Academy's endorsement of him, as an international authority in his field.

When he came to the table displaying the posts, the picture was more serious still. According to the table, Government had three professors at present: Roy Beadle, Fernando Obscurando, and Medway – Bruce Whitelist having already left for greener pastures and bigger lunches. Now came the kicker. According to the proposal, the three professors would be reduced to one.

What were his chances of being the survivor? There were major points in his favour: he was the best-published of the three and he had the imprimatur of the Academy. You might have thought his case was promising. But there was a strong 'narrative' – to use a term currently favoured by the bureaucracy – running against him. He was just the kind of senior academic Murdo wanted to get rid of because his salary would be a significant saving – he could be replaced by two teaching-specialist Eloi. And where was he in the dimension of research that now really mattered, the winning of external grant money? Nowhere. In addition, there was the not inconsiderable matter of Ethel's hostility. She could be counted on to take any opportunity of ridding herself of Medway. His Academy fellowship would count for nothing – Ethel would not even acknowledge it.

Of course, Beadle was another target of Ethel's animosity, and neither Beadle nor Obscurando were different from Medway in the paucity of their grants. But Obscurando had one asset that made him by far the outstanding candidate – indeed, virtually guaranteed his survival: his role in the spousal package that secured the appointment of his wife, Professor Fledermaus. Murdo needed Obscurando because he needed Fledermaus. He did not need Beadle or Medway. They had made the mistake of choosing as partners people Murdo did not want to be college deans.

It seemed to Medway fairly clear that he was gone – Beadle too. A deeper question was whether he really wanted the job now. He had never asked himself this before. His unquestioned goal had been to keep working. This was how he'd written his books: he just kept plodding away no matter what. Sarah kept telling him that he did not have to be there and kept wishing he was not; she said the same thing when Medway told her the news that evening. But it took Ethel to make him wonder if Sarah was right. This was the ultimate restructuring, it seemed to Medway: not the absurd rearrangement of administrative furniture or even the culling of those unfortunates who failed to fit some arbitrary profile, but the conversion of people who were born to be academics, who had heard the music of the spheres of scholarship and devoted themselves to the university life body and soul, into hollowed-out beings for whom the university was an object of loathing.

But there was still enough uncertainty in the situation to make him unsure that he was quite finished. One professorial post would remain, and it was still open to Medway to apply for it. It seemed to him unlikely that he would get it, but who knew? Even if he failed, he would continue to be paid while they were deciding what to do with him.

Medway needed advice. The following morning he knocked on Plume's door but, unsurprisingly, got no answer. He decided he could not face whatever farrago of rumour, speculation and smug self-interest Pleonexia might serve up. What about Beadle? In theory he was Medway's rival for the remaining post, but in reality he was a fellow-sufferer. Ethel probably saw Beadle as a rival centre of authority, which in an informal sense he was, so this was an excellent chance to rid herself of a secretly turbulent academic. Medway decided he had nothing to lose, so he continued down the corridor and knocked on Beadle's door. Sure enough, the oracle was in, manning his post in defiance of all the odds and of reason itself.

'Have a seat, Geoff,' said Beadle. Medway could see straight away that he was going to be sympathetic.

Beadle was also adamant in his own determination to hang on to the bitter end. 'Make them drive in the nails,' he urged Medway. Once again, it was unclear why Beadle would bother clinging to office, apart from a grim vow to outlast Ethel if it was the last thing he did.

'I admire your fortitude, Roy,' said Medway. 'But I have to say I'm in two minds. I'm not sure I'm ready to go, but I'm not sure I really want to stay either. I've just about had enough of this place.'

Beadle nodded and, astonishingly, proceeded to recite something from memory:

> Two roads diverged in a yellow wood,
> And sorry I could not travel both
> And be one traveler, long I stood
> And looked down one as far I could
> To where it bent in the undergrowth

With an effort, Medway recognised Robert Frost. Coming from Beadle, it was as if Medway's mother had suddenly quoted a section of Wittgenstein's *Tractatus*.

Seeing Medway's amazement, Beadle explained: 'There's more to life than public policy and the politics of Leichardt. When I'm at home, I like to read.'

Medway had always assumed that Beadle's life *was* entirely about public policy and the politics of Leichardt. It came as a revelation that this apparently austere and utilitarian character could also have such a completely different side to his personality. There had been little evidence of it when Beadle was in his leadership positions. It was as if, under those conditions, he had decided that any hint of humanity would be taken as a sign of weakness. But there really had been a human being with recognisable feelings concealed there all along. It was strange but oddly comforting.

Beadle also offered practical counsel. 'Before you make any decision, seek absolute clarity.' Medway saw what Beadle meant. He was probably finished, but maybe, just maybe, he wasn't. The uncertainty surrounding him was like a thick liquid in which he was suspended, thrashing abut helplessly.

Medway thanked Beadle and returned to his room. He paced about, his face a field of electrical tensions, trying to think it through. There was, as a result of the University's concern that the affected staff's suffering should not be prolonged, very little time to decide. The change proposal was published on a Tuesday, and redundancy applications had to be submitted by close of business on the following Monday. Those who were interested in taking redundancy would be granted a brief interview with Ethel on Thursday or Friday. The upshot was that Medway had six days to decide whether to end a career of twenty-three years, assisted by an audience with Ethel lasting fifteen minutes. The windows on the opposite side of the quad were as blank and anonymous as ever, while down in the desert courtyard the gnomes were still there. Did they hint at the possibility of an alternative life or just a fantasy world?

Seizing a piece of paper, Medway set about constructing a table of alternatives. On the side of getting out there were a number of powerful considerations: Ethel's vindictive hostility, the lack of respect from the University, the destruction of his undergraduate courses, the tedium of some of the 'teaching' he now had to do, the impossible research expectations, the devaluing of publications in favour of 'inputs', the visceral dislike he had developed of any kind of administration because of the arbitrariness, absurdity and outright malice of the policies. It was also a great source of comfort that money wasn't an issue. If he took redundancy, there would be a payout equivalent to two years' salary (after tax). When this was added to his superannuation account, he would have the amount he was aiming at for retirement. And think of the things he might do if he was liberated from the life-sapping burdens of Leichardt. It had more than once occurred to him that he might get a lot more proper academic work done if only he could avoid the University. Perhaps Jose Escondido had been right after all. Adding up all these factors, he had a powerful desire to seize the redundancy payment before it could get away.

And yet. It was hard to let go after so many years. Part of him could still not believe this was happening. In particular, it was hard to accept being shown the door by the likes of Murdo, Ethel and Sediment. Why should he do them the favour of going quietly? Maybe he should emulate Beadle and force them to drive in the nails. It was not even clear that Ethel really wanted him gone. Perhaps he had misread the signs and she had no intention of getting rid of him. It again occurred to him that maybe she just wanted to torture him for a while – that would be in character. She had said nothing explicitly, so he did not know for certain.

Medway decided to try one last, tentative sounding. He would put in an expression of interest for a voluntary redundancy. That would not commit him to leaving but it would entitle him to an interview with Ethel. He would use the interview to gauge whether she had any interest at all in keeping him. If she hadn't, he would apply for the payout. It seemed like a sensible compromise.

19

INTO THE LIGHT

On Friday morning Medway presented himself at the maw of the Labyrinth. A functionary came out and conducted him to the Bunker, where Doris was occupying her usual position, guarding the door like Cerberus at the entrance to Hades. Millicent, protesting loudly, was being ushered out, and Medway was ushered in without delay. There was a sense of widgets revolving on a conveyor-belt.

Ethel was seated at the meeting table with Sediment by her side. A disturbing sense of occasion was signalled when, uncharacteristically, Ethel rose from her chair and limply held out her hand, cold and flaccid, as if presenting Medway with a dead fish. He recalled the custom of shaking hands with your executioner. There was no eye contact and Ethel seemed subdued. Could she possibly be embarrassed, even frightened? Sediment thrust forward his ursine paw more vigorously. Medway shook it and took no further notice of him. Everything depended on the organ-grinder, not the monkey. They sat.

'So, you've decided to take voluntary redundancy,' said Ethel, still looking down at her papers.

'No, I haven't decided that yet' replied Medway. 'I'm thinking of taking redundancy but at this stage I've only submitted an expression of interest.'

Ethel looked up, squinting fiercely, engaged for the first time. It was evident that the possibility that Medway might be trying to stay had caused real alarm. This in itself was revealing.

'Oh,' she replied, 'these sessions are only for people who are taking redundancy. There's been some mistake. It's not our mistake. These interviews are arranged by someone in People and Culture.' As always, if there was an error, Ethel could not be responsible for it.

'Would you mind if I briefly go through what I'm doing at the moment, just to make sure you have the facts?' Medway asked.

'Oh, we have all the relevant facts but yes, I suppose, go ahead.' Ethel glanced at her watch.

Medway proceeded to outline his teaching, research and administration. On the teaching side, in particular, he wanted to remind Ethel that he was now responsible for three core courses in the Graduate Program. His suspicion was that she associated him only with the doomed 'small courses' in undergraduate political theory and might not realise that he was also teaching postgraduate courses that had good enrolments and made money. He wanted to see if, when she heard this, she would show any surprise or interest.

Not a flicker. She had gone back to looking down at her papers. He tried a different tack.

'I noticed from the change proposal,' he said, 'that you don't see political theory as one of the strengths of the Government section. Does that mean you have no interest in retaining political theory specialists on the staff?'

'Not necessarily. Political theory has its place.'

'Let me ask this, then. If I took redundancy, wouldn't that weaken the capacity of the section to maintain the political theory part of the program?'

'Not necessarily. You're not the only political theorist, there's also Professor Obscurando.'

That said it all.

'So,' Medway pursued, 'do you think there's any point in my applying for one of the posts?'

'That's for you to judge,' Ethel replied. 'The criteria are set out in the job descriptions.' She went on to give a mechanical review of some wretched 'skills matching' system that was being used to assess the applications, but now it was Medway's turn to stop listening. His question, about whether there was any chance of his staying, had been answered.

Fine. The prospect of leaving suddenly sounded wonderful. No more classes and marking; no more daily harassment by the administration, or worse still being forced to be part of the administration himself; pursuing his own research without having to worry about grants; above all, no more dealings with Ethel.

'Thank you. I need to think about this further, but it's likely I'll apply for redundancy.' He was also thinking that, if he was quick, he could lunge across the table with his pen and stab Ethel right in the squint. This might be his last chance.

But it was too late. 'All right,' said Ethel, 'but if you're applying, you need to do that by close of business on Monday. Now, I'm afraid our fifteen minutes are up and we have our next appointment.' Without waiting for any response from Medway she turned away and began a conversation with Sediment.

The next widget was waiting on the conveyor-belt. Medway left the Bunker and was escorted from the Labyrinth.

***

It was Monday morning and Medway was in his office, pacing about again. His face was lighting up like a switchboard but he had decisions to make. If he was going to take a package he had to say so today. Alternatively, he could wait, Beadle-like, for Ethel to drive in the nails. But did he really want to go through a painful round of interviews only to be told that he was not up to the standard of Obscurando?

He decided to go for a walk along the corridor to clear his head. He was passing Beadle's room when it occurred to him to run his thoughts past the sage if he was on duty. He was, as always, bowed over his desk at the far end of the over-sized room.

'You know,' said Beadle, 'I think you could stay if you wanted to. Even if Ethel rejected you for any of the positions, and even if you were eventually deemed unredeployable, you would still be able to fight.'

'Really, how?' Medway was intrigued.

'Did Ethel give you a performance review last year?'

'No, I was expecting one, of course, but it never happened.'

'I didn't think so,' said Beadle. 'There've been other cases.'

'I assumed she was distracted by other matters.'

'No doubt, but that's a serious procedural mistake,' said Beadle, a wintry smile eating into his lugubrious features. 'Every staff member is entitled to an annual performance review. Only then can management say you were duly warned of whatever inadequacy you've allegedly shown in your work. It was Ethel's obligation to review your performance. If she didn't, she neglected to perform one of her most important duties. She deprived you of a process that was, if not exactly a pleasure, your right.'

Medway recalled what a serious matter this had been in the case of Jose Escondido, who had almost managed to fight his dismissal because of a similar omission. Jose didn't quite succeed because his non-review was really his own doing, caused by his being AWOL. Medway, on the other hand, had been present on campus and available all year; Ethel had simply not bothered with him.

Beadle was a genius! However annoying he'd been in the past (and his annoyance quotient hadn't been negligible), the man had turned out to be a treasure. His argument had the added attraction that it would neatly impale Ethel on the kind of administrative barb that she delighted in applying to others. If the ploy worked, Medway would achieve a quite delicious form of poetic justice. He could yet succeed in delivering a blinding jab to the Ethelian squint.

Thanking Beadle profusely, Medway continued on his walk, following the corridor around the building back towards his room. He felt elated, like someone who had been reconciled to his execution only to be reprieved at the last moment. He would survive this. And he would survive Ethel. Eventually, the obese harridan would retire and Medway would still be in possession, like a Sphagnumian cockroach. Perhaps the College would then get better leadership but, in any case, it would be worth it just to outlast Old Squinty. O frabjous day! Callooh callay!

Then, being Medway, he began to think again. Pausing at a window with a view of the Hayek South quad, he looked out onto the dusty, carceral enclosure. He imagined tumbleweed blowing past the hunched, fugitive figures of those who had not met the research expectations. A hot, fetid wind howled through the bleached bones of former deans. If he stayed, this would continue to be his life. How, he asked himself, would he feel then?

He would feel cheated of the redundancy money. It was hard to let go but if he managed to stay he would feel worse still. Like others before him, he really had had enough. Enough of teaching students who couldn't write a decent sentence in English (this included many of the locals as well as the internationals and actually applied to some staff members too – Obscurando and Whelper came to mind). Enough of chasing impossible research expectations that had nothing to do with whether the research was worthwhile.

Enough of performing thankless administrative tasks that took him away from his academic work. Enough of having his life governed by the University's obsession with making money. Enough of working for a college led by a sadist and a university presided over by a bully.

By the time he was back in his room he was less elated but had made up his mind. Brilliant and tempting though Beadle's arguments were, he would not pursue them. What *would* he do? Doing nothing was still a possibility. He could let the process take its course and be fairly sure that he would be rejected after the interviews. But what if, against all expectations, he was retained? That faint possibility was a risk that, he realised, he was unwilling to take. He had glimpsed a narrow chink in the dark wall of the panopticon, and nothing was going to stop him from bursting through into the daylight.

He sat down at the computer and typed out his application for voluntary redundancy. His finger hovered over the send button for a moment, then pressed it.

***

Medway would not be the only departure from the College of Non-Sciences. Wielded by Ethel, Murdo's axe accounted for several past stalwarts. For a start, just about anyone who had ever criticised or even raised any questions about Ethel's rule was cleaned out. This accounted, for example, for that troublemaker from Law, Alex Euripides. From the Government section, Millicent went unquietly into the night, declaring that Ethel was 'a running dog of capitalism.' Whelper was only too delighted to take a package, since he had little interest in continuing in any case and had only been waiting for an opportunity to collect some severance money.

Among the survivors were Professors Cardigan and Obscurando, both untouchable for different reasons. Plume and Pleonexia would continue to provide their proven leadership. Two further survivors were more surprising. Beadle outwitted Ethel, cleverly taking advantage of procedural errors made by her underlings to preserve himself for another two years. Once again, it was unclear why he would want to do that, apart from sheer bloody-mindedness.

More strangely still, Putz, that famous non-publisher, yet again retained his job. Not only that, he was kept on not as a teaching specialist – if there was ever a case for such a conversion it was Putz – but in a balanced teaching-and-research post. So, while scores of regular publishers would be seen no more, an inveterate non-performer in that area would be rewarded. To be fair, Putz had two important things going for him. First, there was his impressive track record in exploiting the Union's defensive services. Ethel had received a couple of bloody noses in that regard and was probably wary of getting another one. Second, there was Putz's relatively lowly rank as a Lecturer – he was still on the entry level after twenty years. By cunningly underperforming for decades, he had avoided promotion to the more senior ranks which, because they were better paid, were more vulnerable to the reprofiling process.

Well, thought Medway, the survivors were welcome to it.

20

GRAND
REMONSTRANCE

The moment of the great Council meeting arrived, a bright
early-summer's day. The fate of the staff was sealed anyway,
but at least, thanks to Professor Cardigan's efforts, they would
get a public hearing of their grievances: something like the
Grand Remonstrance of 1641 or FDR's 'day of infamy'
speech. Being listened to was another matter – that obviously
wouldn't happen – but they would have their day in court.
Medway felt relaxed, expansive. He would be leaving anyway.
He was just interested to hear what the staff's representatives
would say, and how Goldfinger and Murdo would respond.

Shortly after lunch, crowds of academics, especially from
Non-Sciences, streamed down the hill towards the Milton
Friedman Building. By hallowed tradition, meetings of the
Council always took place there, in the old Council Room
located on the top floor. Murdo would have to emerge from
his Citadel and enter the territory of the great Chifley
Occupation of 1970. Ethel said she would be remaining in her

Bunker, but not, Medway was sure, from any fear of reprisals. Neither of them would have been too concerned that there would be a similar uprising this time. The neoliberal management systems of the University had achieved such total hegemony that revolt was inconceivable.

The scene on the way down the hill and outside the Friedman Building was festive. Lecturers in English and philosophy marched with sociologists, political scientists, social workers and lawyers. There were professional staff and casuals, even smatterings of scientists. All of Leichardt was represented.

Beadle would not be present – these days he tended to keep out of the spotlight, preferring to advise behind the scenes. But at a meeting of the Government group beforehand, he had counselled them not to look or behave 'like a rabble.'

'Don't give them that satisfaction,' he said. 'Wear your blazer.' On the one hand this was the annoyingly authentic voice of Beadle the head prefect, on the other they could see his point. Medway, however, would not be wearing his sodding blazer.

Plume had defied expectations, left his sick-bed and was present, blazer correct. Few other blazers were in evidence, but the gathering was scarcely a rabble. The mood was, on the whole, buoyant, exuding the sense of solidarity that crowds can generate. It reminded Medway of the street protests of the 1970s and 80s. In those days, protest rallies were routine: university students used to march downtown to Parliament several times a year. When Medway arrived at Leichardt in the mid-90s, the culture of protest was somewhat weaker but still in evidence. Sarah used to make an annual pilgrimage into the city along with her teacher colleagues to object to the latest assaults on public education. They would stand on the steps of State Parliament and chant, 'Teachers united will never be defeated!' Now such events were much less frequent. The teachers had been defeated, along with everyone else. Mrs Thatcher's message that 'there is no alternative' had permeated everywhere.

Yet here they were, converging en masse on a site of oppression. There was an atmosphere of carnival, a licensed inversion of the customary order. The staff's representatives would be listened to – or at any rate heard – and the staff would be on hand to see that happen. It was all very exciting.

Medway followed the crowd down to CHQ. Arriving at the Friedman Building, everyone climbed the stairs to the third floor. A long passage led past the Committee Room, where Medway had nodded through many meetings, and the former offices of the Vice-Chancellor and Deputy Vice-Chancellor (Academic), now deemed insufficiently splendid and used for other purposes. At the end of the corridor was the Council Room.

Entering, Medway found yet another familiar place: he'd suffered through numerous meetings here too. It was a long room dominated by a huge, coffin-shaped table, the centre of which was hollow so that technicians could get ready access to the audio-visual equipment located in it on a central island. Along the sides of the room, rows of windows presented views of the city to the north and Murdo's Citadel next door.

At each end, the chamber was decorated by wooden panelling featuring portraits of the University's former Chancellors and Vice-Chancellors. Medway recognised some of the latter – among them the physicist who had come up with Leichardt's tree-of-knowledge design, Murdo's predecessor, Professor Pound, and Pound's predecessor, a humourless sociologist who had once turned Medway down for promotion. The rude forefathers and foremothers of the hamlet.

The room was already packed to overflowing with members of staff. Most of them were ranged along the windows, some seated on chairs but many perched on the windowsills. Others stood around the entrance to the room, making it hard to get through. With some difficulty Medway managed to edge into the room and find a space where he could lean against a window near the door. There was a roar of conversation. He spotted people he knew in the crowd: Nick talking to someone from the Union, Plume coughing into a handkerchief, Pleonexia gossiping with her friends. Whelper, in complete corporate ensemble, was staring adoringly at the Chancellor and Vice-Chancellor, who were already sitting in state at the far end of the great table. Professors Tennyson and Toynbee were deep in conversation. Millicent shouted from the other side of the room and Nola the Flamingo waved. Another figure lurked surreptitiously, a Make Leichardt Great cap pulled down well over his eyes. It was Byron Scape. What was he doing there?

Goldfinger, as chair of the Council, occupied the place of honour, with Murdo scowling at his right hand. Around the table were ranged people who Medway took to be the Council members – all resplendent in their blazers. About the ordinary Council members Medway knew nothing except that, aside from the two staff and student representatives, they seemed to be lickspittles of the regime.

Beaming around the room, Goldfinger seemed to be under the impression that the throng had come to congratulate him on his brilliant work. Murdo looked more nervous. He was confronted, outside the Citadel, by a roomful of those whose careers he was ending. He fidgeted in his chair, like an egg boiling in a saucepan, his eyes widening.

Eventually Goldfinger brought the meeting to order and the hubbub diminished to a low susurrus, then a tense silence.

'Welcome to this meeting of the Leichardt University Council,' said Goldfinger. 'Today the Council has important matters to discuss concerning the current restructure, and that discussion will be held in private. But first, we have agreed to hear statements from Professor Kate Cardigan and two of her colleagues. Each of them will have three minutes.'

Medway was reminded of the three-minute thesis and his ordeal at the Academy.

'Members of staff are welcome to stay while those statements are being made, but at the conclusion of the statements we ask that you leave so that we can continue with our confidential deliberations. It is not possible or desirable to debate the issue, but we will listen to what your spokesmen – er, spokespeople – have to say. Those comments will be taken on board, please be assured. We are all here to ensure that the University prospers, and that its development aligns with its agreed aspirations. Over to you, Professor Cardigan.'

Cardigan stood up and walked to the foot of the table, facing Goldfinger and Murdo. Slightly built, dignified and intense, she had opted for a black business jacket instead of the corporate blazer. Her iron-grey hair was tied back severely from her forehead. Cardigan positively radiated all that was best, brightest and most earnest in the traditions of Leichardt academia.

'I'm going to speak about the reputational damage caused by the current changes,' she began. 'Staff morale is low, the lowest I've ever seen. This discontent is common knowledge throughout the State, even nationally, and evidence of it can be seen everywhere. It can be seen in the University's reluctance to publish the results of the *Your Say* survey, in the open letter from staff to the Vice-Chancellor which has attracted 250 signatures, in the numerous petitions that have appeared online, in the outpouring of commentary on social media, and in the attendance we see today.'

Goldfinger maintained his placid, self-satisfied expression but Murdo continued to wriggle in his seat, his eyes protruding, a study in discomfort.

'The risk in low morale is poor performance,' Cardigan continued. 'The University's senior management places a lot of emphasis on achieving a high quality of staff performance, yet its policies threaten to undermine that goal.'

There was a solid round of applause from the staff. Murdo sat back in his chair with his arms folded tightly across his chest, trying to control himself.

'The reason for all this discontent is pretty obvious: the staff have been treated appallingly,' said Cardigan. 'Here are some of the words that have been used to describe that treatment: heartless, cruel, disrespectful, unnecessary. People have been disempowered not only by the changes themselves but also by the haste with which the changes are being introduced. Staff are also exasperated by the senior management's lack of transparency, lack of willingness to justify its decisions, and, in all probability, lack of understanding of the nature and consequences of its own actions. Time and again, questions have been raised that senior management has not been able to answer.'

Murmurs of confirmation came from the audience. Murdo was now sitting forward in his chair as if about to respond but unable to do so. He must have agreed, after that disastrous television interview, to let Goldfinger do the talking. But he was gripping a pen as he would a non-grant-accumulating academic he was trying to strangle.

'The Vice-Chancellor,' Cardigan went on, 'has said that only a relatively few staff members will be affected by the changes. We estimate that over two hundred staff fall within the official affected category. These include many people who have been highly successful in their fields and have devoted a large part of their working lives to Leichardt.'

Further murmurs of support rippled about.

'But beyond the narrow meaning assigned to the label "affected" by the bureaucracy, *all* the staff are affected by this restructure.'

A huge explosion of applause followed. In spite of his general mood of exhaustion and ambivalence, Medway found it quite moving. Apparently he was not alone and there were others, even people like Cardigan whose jobs were not at risk, who cared about what was happening to those awaiting execution.

'Let me elaborate briefly. First, the supposedly unaffected are distressed at the way their colleagues have been treated; second, there is the possibility of further restructures in the not too distant future; third, departments and units have been changed without any adequate rationale; fourth, whole programs have been altered in ways that raise accreditation issues.'

Medway had to suppress a bitter laugh at the mention of accreditation. He also saw that Murdo was now glaring directly at Cardigan, as if trying to silence her with a malign telekinetic energy. Murdo's emotions, which usually described a tight arc between irritation and rage, were evidently threatening to veer off the dial.

Cardigan was impervious. 'To add insult to injury, the staff's only real protection, the Union, has been blamed for prolonging the process. Senior management's message seems to be that the staff should accept whatever is decided because fairness takes too long.'

Murdo was evidently beside himself now, his bulbous eyes springing out of his head as if on stalks. There was another break for applause. Cardigan's allotted time was almost up, and Medway could see her gathering herself for one last effort.

'I had a dream the other night,' she said. My God, thought Medway, is this going to be like Martin Luther King? Perhaps Cardigan had a vision of a rosy future in which staff got along with management and everyone was judged according to the content of their teaching and publication rather than the quantity of money in their research input account. But no, Cardigan's dream was different.

'I dreamed that someone was chainsawing all the trees on campus. The rich forest that was the Leichardt academic community is being clear-felled.' Someone? Everyone knew who that was. And the image of the chainsaw was richly suggestive. Murdo would probably reply that he was only pruning the tree of knowledge, especially the dead wood in its lower branches. Philosophy might have Ockham's Razor; Leichardt had Murdo's chainsaw. But the image of the Vice-Chancellor as Leatherface, sporting a mask hand-made out of human skins, seemed more to the point.

Realising she was out of time, Cardigan finally wound up quickly. 'This is a huge mistake. Thank you for listening.'

A massive round of applause followed and continued for a long time. For the staff, it was a rare opportunity to express themselves emotionally in the face of Leichardt's impersonal machinery of control and elimination. For Murdo, it must have been like a drumming, pounding negation of all he stood for.

And it wasn't over yet: the other two Distinguished Professors were still to come. The first of these, Maggie Dworkin, from Law, argued that the University's process had been so hurried that it had failed to provide procedural fairness to those affected by its decisions, as required by its governing Act of Parliament. Finally, Professor Morpheus, from Psychology, spelled out what everyone already believed, that the real motivation behind the whole catastrophe was a desperate desire to improve the University's research rankings. This was, he said, a short-term policy that would come to grief as soon as the rankings agencies realised that universities like Leichardt were gaming the system.

Again there was a cacophonous round of applause, cheering and stamping of feet.

The thunder diminishing at last, Goldfinger thanked the three Distinguished Professors for their comments. If he'd left it at that, he would have been fine. He had, after all, said at the start that there would be no debate, that the Council would listen to what Cardigan and the others had to say and then deliberate in private. So, he could now say simply that it was time for the private deliberations to commence, and the public part of the meeting was closed.

But the words of the professors had left wounds, and Goldfinger could not resist picking at them.

'I wish to make a couple of points,' he said. 'Today you have heard one-half of the story. The other half is that the Council and I have a responsibility to make sure that the University succeeds.'

'By pushing out hundreds of competent people,' someone interjected.

Goldfinger ignored the interjection. 'We are faced with serious challenges,' he continued. 'These are mostly not of our making. They include changes of government policy, such as the decision of the Gillard government to change the whole basis of the higher education sector to one driven by demand. To meet these challenges, we need to be increasingly agile so that we can deliver on the aspirations of the University and the career aspirations of the staff, and so that we can maximise student experience.'

How many times had the staff heard this kind of claptrap before? The word 'agile' alone was enough to trigger spasms of nausea. Basically, it was code for the idea that employers could do what they liked and employees had to do whatever they were told. Hence, it was unclear how the University's new agility was going to advance 'the career aspirations of the staff.' Numerous careers were being ended prematurely. And what on earth did it mean to say that the University should 'maximise student experience'? Was student experience something that could be quantified, so that student X might have 10 units of experience and student Y 20 units? It was like something out of Obscurando. Finally, it was a mystery how the students would benefit by losing their teachers.

'Change is necessary,' Goldfinger droned on, 'if we don't want the University to be marginalised. I'm tempted to quote badly the words of our first Vice-Chancellor: "Sometimes you have to be brave to get where you want to be."'

Losing patience with this drivel, the audience erupted in groans of disbelief and exclamations of derision punctuated by cries of 'Shame!' and 'No confidence!' Murdo tried folding his arms again but he still looked as though unseen demons were jabbing him with burning brands. Perhaps trigeminal facial neuralgia was setting in, thought Medway. One could only hope.

Goldfinger plodded stubbornly on. He had a lot of experience of facing down angry shareholders and incensed environmental regulators, and he was not going to be derailed by a bunch of pointy-headed academics.

'You need to see it in the broader picture. I won't ask you to leave convinced you're wrong, but there's another side to the matter.'

The groans and exclamations continued. They seemed to provoke Goldfinger to go further.

'Actually,' he added, as if an epiphany had suddenly illuminated his universe, 'I totally disagree that there is any effort on behalf of management or Council to try to bump up the rankings.'

Howls of laughter followed that would have been welcomed by any professional comedian. But onwards Goldfinger laboured.

'We do have to improve our rankings because our future depends on them. But I do not accept the insinuation that we are doing it for short-term gain.' Doing what? He'd just said that they weren't trying to bump up the rankings. Now he seemed to be saying they were trying to bump up the rankings but this was justified.

'I'd now like to make some comments of my own,' Goldfinger continued. Oddly, it seemed that this was what he'd been doing already, but on he went, descending deeper into the hole he was digging for himself.

'Critical assertions have been made against the Vice-Chancellor and myself. Against the Vice-Chancellor it has been said that the restructure process has been instituted in order to serve his personal agenda, that it serves short-term ends, that it is ill-conceived, and that it is not in the best interests of the University. Those assertions are false. The

Vice-Chancellor is personally committed to the University and its success, to the interests of its staff, and to the maximisation of the student experience.'

'Absolute rubbish!' someone interjected. Murdo winced but Goldfinger was undeterred. People were beginning to move towards the exits, but Goldfinger blundered onwards like a somnambulist.

'Discussions about the current changes have been taking place over the past seven years. They began under the previous Vice-Chancellor. The current Vice-Chancellor has been appointed to continue those changes. Again, the changes have been driven by alterations in government policy going back to the Gillard period. The changes are necessary. If we didn't make them, you'd come to us in three years' time and ask why they had not been made.'

'But we won't be here, fuckwit, because you'll have sacked us!' a critic sagely observed.

Medway had joined the press of people shuffling out of the room and was working his way past the foot of the great table when he realised that, for the first time, he had a clear view of Goldfinger and Murdo at the top. Unusually, for him, he decided to seize the moment. He summoned his lecturing voice before he could second-guess himself.

'May I ask a question?' he began, then ploughed on straight away before he got the wrong answer. 'You said you'd take our comments on board, but how can you do that when you've just said we're wrong? You said the Council would take account of what we had to say, then you explicitly rejected what we had to say.'

'You're talking in absolutes,' Goldfinger responded, 'and nothing is absolute.'

'But you said you "totally disagree" with us.'

Goldfinger finally saw that he was not making things better. He had declared that there was not going to be a debate and then entered into a debate. Now at last he tried to extricate himself.

'I'm not here to tell you you're wrong,' he said. 'We'll take your comments on board.'

But it was too late. Goldfinger had taken his badgering hypocrisy a step too far and something snapped in the mood of the crowd.

What happened next happened so quickly that Medway could not immediately grasp everything that was going on. He was conscious only of a sudden uproar at the head of the table, and of the formation of two groups, like a pair of rugby mauls or football rucks, around the Chancellor and Vice-Chancellor. It was only later, with the help of the video recording that was being made of the meeting, eventually available on YouTube, that the sequence of events became clearer.

To begin with, violent hands were laid on Goldfinger. Two large men from the Sports Physiology unit dragged him from his chair and flung him on his back over the table. One of the men leapt into the well of the table, in a display that Goldfinger might have approved in another context as 'agile.' He stretched the Chancellor's arms above his head while his comrade secured one of Goldfinger's legs. They were joined by an art historian who took hold of the other leg.

Next, someone from Languages produced a Make Leichardt Great T-shirt and draped it over Goldfinger's face. He then picked up a nearby carafe of water and proceeded to waterboard Goldfinger, using the method that had become familiar from the activities of the CIA in various parts of the world. Goldfinger coughed, spluttered, choked, and made muffled bellowing noises but the treatment continued.

'Stop, you're torturing him!' implored some humanitarian, possibly Cardigan.

'He's been torturing us!' replied the lecturer from Languages.

Half-hearted attempts at intervention were made by other Council members, but they were clearly terrified that they might be next. This was perhaps a salutary taste for them of what it must be like to be on the redeployment list, it occurred to Medway. Soon, most of them had either hastily gathered up their laptops and fled, or else been ushered out by hostile academics.

'There go the money-changers!' someone shouted. Medway identified Millicent.

Meanwhile, Murdo suffered a fate similar to Goldfinger's. After briefly trying to liberate the Chancellor, he was seized by a team consisting of Professors Tennyson and Toynbee and the entire Philosophy unit – now down to two people and due to be reduced soon to one teaching-specialist post. Inspired by what was being done to Goldfinger, Murdo's captors flung him over the big table too. His arms were more powerful than Goldfinger's, so this time two people were needed in the well of the table to hold them. This task was given to the two philosophers, but at the last minute one of them was thrust aside and replaced by a powerful figure in a Make Leichardt Great cap – Byron Scape. Professors Tennyson and Toynbee held onto Murdo's legs, Toynbee accidentally dislodging an Italian shoe and throwing it casually over his shoulder. Murdo did not take this reversal of fortune well, shrieking threats at his assailants, Scape in particular, his eyes bulging alarmingly.

Such is the conditioning of the academic mind to search for originality that, in their choice of chastisement, Murdo's tormentors selected a different method from that applied to the Chancellor. Rather than thrown onto his back, Murdo was pushed down onto his face. An associate professor of Nursing – Medway knew her slightly from some committee – moved round behind him and, reaching forward, wrenched Murdo's trousers down to his knees. She did the same with Murdo's underpants. With a flourish, she then produced a glossy document and rolled it up tightly. Shouting '*Sic semper tyrannis*', she thrust it hard into Murdo's bottom. Finally, she struck a match and applied it to the uppermost end of the projecting roll. Murdo emitted a loud wail of agony and his eyeballs threatened to exit from his head.

Medway sensed that the identity of the document was significant, but from the other end of the room he could not see clearly what it was, although he could guess. Only later, when he was able to watch the YouTube video, did he confirm his supposition when the camera-operator zoomed in on the spectacle at the moment of insertion.

It was a copy of the Target 1% brochure.

21

IN THE RUINS

The remainder of the action that day is familiar from news reports, police statements and trial proceedings, so it need not be rehearsed in detail. Suffice it to say that the riot that began in the Council Room spilled out through the Milton Friedman Building and onto the CHQ square. There, a large number of staff broke into the Citadel and ransacked the offices of Murdo and his myrmidons. Pleonexia was among those who entered the Vice-Chancellor's suite in search of the fabled hit list. The great Chifley Occupation of 1970 was nothing by comparison.

Security eventually turned up but they were powerless to stop a large, rampaging mob of academics, most of whom would shortly lose their jobs and had little more to hope or fear from the University. Throngs of lecturers capered around CHQ singing, to the tune of 'Campdown Races,'

> Murdo takes it up the arse,
> Doo da, doo da,

Murdo takes it up the arse,
All de doo da day.

Experts in postcolonial studies objected, but the singers were having too much fun to take any notice.

A good deal of physical damage soon occurred. Rocks were thrown at CHQ's big video screen by people from a range of disciplines whose methodologies emphasised reading. Murdo's Citadel was spray-painted by lecturers from Visual Arts, who used the traditional words for such occasions – 'wanker', 'overpaid prick', 'neoliberal arsehole' and so forth – but set these in beautiful designs, the lettering either chunkily monumental or swirlingly dynamic, depending on the tastes of the artist. The traditional words were supplemented by others more specifically influenced by recent events – 'liar', 'cheat', 'ball-tamperer' – even more pleasingly presented, featuring illustrations of Pinocchio in cricket whites sharpening his long nose with sandpaper.

Only the bust of Aristotle, although still sporting its Make Leichardt Great cap, was spared any further indignity, perhaps recognised by the rioters as a fellow-sufferer.

Medway watched some of this but had soon seen enough. He set out on the long climb to his car, which was parked as usual at Ultima Thule. About half-way up, as he was approaching the upper branches of the tree of knowledge, he paused and looked back. He could see a column of black smoke rising over the centre of the university. Sirens sounded in the distance. Then there was a sudden flash and the annihilating sound of a terrific explosion. Medway could feel the concussion where he was standing. A volcanic tongue of flame shot into the sky from the direction of CHQ.

The restructure had taken an unexpected turn.

***

In the wake of the riot and explosion, it would take Leichardt some time to recover. Both the Milton Friedman Building and Murdo's Citadel were now smoking ruins. According to the police, a group of revolutionary hold-outs from Sociology had fire-bombed them with Molotov cocktails. The design of the Citadel, in particular, proved less impregnable than had been supposed, because the flames had somehow reached the gas lines, resulting in a massive fireball that briefly illuminated the surrounding suburbs before causing a local power blackout.

Murdo did not survive. The media, forgetting the Scape revelations, mourned the passing of a 'cricket legend and university reformer.' His family, most of whom had seen Murdo only occasionally in recent years, accepted a state funeral service, which was held at the city's test cricket venue. In front of a crowd of 50,000, Murdo's casket did a circuit of the ground, resting on the tray of his Lamborghini truck. On its lid was his baggy green, together with his Make Leichardt Great cap. At the centre of the ground, the wicket was mowed and rolled, and a set of stumps was put in place, as if Murdo was about to take guard. One of his favourite Predators was propped against the stumps, and, in an especially poignant touch, his box was hooked over the off-side bail.

A sequence of loved ones and supporters spoke movingly of the cricketer, the Vice-Chancellor, and the man.

'We have lost a great Australian,' said Jim Dixon. 'Murdo was one of the all-time batting stars, a superb leader who cared about his players and gave everything for the team, and a fine man who set an example of courage, wisdom and rectitude in all his dealings with others.'

'He was a top bloke,' said Murdo's old opening bowler, Dave 'Bodyline' Loader, who broke down and couldn't continue, as had so often been the case during his test career. As he was led away, weeping, he kept looking up to the sky, presumably expecting to see the spirit of Murdo suspended up there.

Finally, Goldfinger, who had amazingly survived, although with burns and other injuries, spoke warmly of Murdo's dedication to the staff of Leichardt. He would be sorely missed and – here some commentators detected a hint of pique in Goldfinger's voice – hard to replace.

***

A problem with violent solutions is that they tend to lead to unpredictable consequences. One thing the Leichardt rioters did not foresee was that, along with Murdo, some one hundred academics also perished. Another thirty seriously injured, and a dozen or so had been arrested and were awaiting trial, some of them in custody.

Most of those killed were people who were in or around the Citadel at the moment of the explosion. These included

Millicent, who was last heard yelling, 'Onward, comrades!' Plume vanished without trace, having picked the wrong day to come to work. Professors Tennyson and Toynbee were also among the missing, as was the two-man Philosophy department and Byron Scape.

The survivors included Professor Cardigan and Nick, who both left the Milton Friedman Building in disgust at the conclusion of Goldfinger's monologue and the start of his waterboarding, and Whelper, who fled when he saw the danger of regime change. Nola the Flamingo also hopped to safety. Pleonexia had a close escape, miraculously dug out of the wreckage some hours later. She was clutching a piece of paper that she claimed was Murdo's legendary hit list, but it turned out to be a receipt for laundry items.

The loss of the deceased academics caused Medway grief in more ways than one. He was, of course, saddened by the death of those he knew personally, and sorry for the families of the others. Was he in fact partly responsible? After all, it was his last-minute intervention in the Council Room that seemed to lead Goldfinger to say those final idiotic words that sent the crowd over the edge. A full answer to that question would require a comprehensive review of the theoretical options in the manner of his deliberations concerning the Scape temptation. He'd torture himself with that later.

In any case he was soon subjected to punishment, whether deserved or not. The disappearance of so many employees from the payroll, especially at the level of associate professor and above, had in one stroke brought about the salary savings and reprofiling that the University had been aiming for in the restructure. Redundancies were no longer required. Everyone's package was cancelled, including Medway's. He could retire anyway, but without the redundancy payout he would fall short of his savings target. To reach it he'd need to work for another two years at least. It was little consolation that Whelper, whose redundancy payout would have been something of a windfall after his research inactivity of recent years, had to stay on too.

Medway found himself staring dismally out at the desert wastes of the Hayek South quad as he worked the Lance Armstrong, contemplating another two years of international students, academic integrity cases, and Ethel.

***

Meanwhile, Goldfinger began his search for a new Vice-Chancellor. The Deputy Vice-Chancellor (Academic), Prudence Climber, was in charge temporarily but, although she was promising, Goldfinger did not think she was quite ready for the full appointment.

Wearily, he arranged for the position to be advertised. Once again, the usual roster of 'leading academics' applied for the job, leaving Goldfinger cold. As weeks went by without the emergence of anyone remotely inspiring, he became desperate. It even crossed his mind to ask Beadle to consider taking the job, before he remembered that Beadle's aspirations no longer aligned with those of the University.

Once again, he was stumped, as he had been after the death of Pound. But once again Lady Barbara helped him to see the way forward. This time, her influence was more directly prescriptive.

'Aurelian,' she said in the firm, admonitory tone in which she said everything, 'isn't it about time that Leichardt had another female Vice-Chancellor. There's been only one in fifty years. Admittedly, that sociologist was a crushing bore, but at least she was a step in the right direction.'

'Do you think so, my dear?'

'I do. What the place needs is a woman's touch. Murdo was all very well, but you need someone who has greater empathy with the staff – the kind of empathy that comes with the female sensibility.'

'It's a wonderful idea, of course, but I can't, off the top of my head, think of anyone who fits the bill. I did consider Prudence Climber, but she's too inexperienced.'

'Just promise me you'll think about it, Aurelian.'

'I promise I will.'

And he did: once again, a seed had been planted. Over the coming days he thought deeply about the matter. Perhaps he had overvalued Murdo's machismo. Maybe the goals of neoliberalism needn't be pursued with maximum brutality; what was important was that they be pursued effectively. On the issue of effectiveness, it had to be admitted – although this was not for public consumption – that Murdo's legacy was disappointing. Target 1% had, frankly, not been a success. Its unpopularity with the staff was only to be expected – many of them needed to be moved on in any case. Somewhat less satisfactorily, quite a number of people ended up being moved on, or moving themselves on, who had actually been contributing well, some of them extremely well. That was unfortunate, but again one had to pay for tough reforms. In the longer view, there were plenty more where these people came from. Despite their own pretensions to distinction, they would be replaced soon enough.

Of greater concern was the fact that Target 1% had failed on its own terms. After Murdo's crusade, Leichardt had actually gone backwards in the rankings. Of course, this embarrassing truth could be camouflaged in public by some agile obfuscation. It was always possible to find some micro-dimension in which Leichardt had done marginally better than its rivals, at any rate within the limited arena of the state. Prudence Climber had recently announced that, out of the state's six universities, Leichardt was 'Number One' in successful employment outcomes for lesbians living with disability.

Nevertheless, the promised land of the top 1% of universities worldwide was further away than ever. Since this goal had been trumpeted so loudly and confidently by Murdo, its non-achievement stood out proportionately as a mark of his failure. He had taken responsibility, and he had fallen short. Had he been worth his $1.2 million salary? To be honest (*in foro interno*), no. Goldfinger did not feel he had had value for money.

So, perhaps Barbara was right that the University needed someone with a different approach. And yes, maybe the key to a better approach was greater empathy with the staff – or at least, not to get too carried way, the appearance of greater empathy. Women were indeed known for their empathetic properties. So, again, perhaps Barbara was also right to recommend the appointment of a woman. The only problem was, who could this be?

Then, at a University function held in Hayek South while CHQ was under reconstruction, Goldfinger fell into conversation with a woman he knew he'd met before but couldn't quite place. She was built on a grand scale and had a habit of squinting out of the corner of her eye. Was she empathetic? She must be; she was a woman. Certainly, she talked sense and had a good attitude. Goldfinger dimly remembered Murdo speaking well of her as, albeit physically repulsive, a useful ally. The seed in Goldfinger's mind was germinating. Why not?

The application came in and, after a friendly interview, Goldfinger rammed it through the Council. The new Vice-Chancellor would be Ethel Korova.

ABOUT THE AUTHOR

Errol Blackadder lives in Australia. He taught in universities in the UK, US and Australia for over thirty years until he was restructured.